CATHARSIS

By Ann Wachter

Copyright © 2011 Ann Wachter

All rights reserved.

ISBN: 1460915690

ISBN-13: 9781460915691

This story is dedicated to my family.

Foreword

I wanted to create a story that would reflect the reality of my life as closely as possible. As I sat and began typing, I soon realized that there were parts of my life that I found difficult to share as well as parts that perhaps would seem inaccurate to my siblings and friends because their perspectives would have been different from mine—as is the case with any human truth. My writing is a condensed recollection of various times and events set forth in a timeline of sorts starting with birth and gradually moving forward as I aged. As events unfolded in my mind, the process of expressing childhood feelings using adult thoughts created epiphanies of understanding which allowed me to not only better articulate my past experiences but to cope with some internal and external struggles I was having in my life of the here and now. Thus, the story in many ways reflects my life today as well as what came from my childhood. The timeline becomes somewhat distorted, however, because actions taken along the way as a child and young adult are not necessarily consistent with when they may have in reality occurred; rather they are placed in terms of my random recollections which is consistent with a more stream-of-consciousness thought process, which, I believe, the vast majority of people utilize when remembering their past experiences. I am now better aware of who I am than when I began my story; its telling has effectively made me feel more secure about facing and interacting with people around me without fear and anxieties that so often overwhelmed me in the past.

When I began writing, I was a sad person who felt that life had passed her by, and that success was something unattainable. I came away from this book a better person, knowing that true success comes from within the boundaries of my own heart, intellect, and imagination, and is never the byproduct of what others say they think about me or my actions unless I agree and allow it to be.

This is a story of my journey to find myself by looking back at my life challenges, setbacks, and lessons learned. I came to realize that during the journey, God placed many good people in my life that sprinkled happy times over the painful ones so as to cover them in a way that protected me until I was prepared to deal with them. I am thus sustained and hope that readers of my story can in some way connect with my life and come to realize that pain is cathartic and an unavoidable necessity of life. In fact, each of us is only an event away from catharsis.

Intro

I once envisioned my life would be *normal*; that is, fame and glory wouldn't be a part of what I thought a happy life should be. A shy, timid personality is central to how I initially project myself to those around me. Not that I intend to be this way; it just happens. Others say the right words, ask the right questions, and project confidence so much easier than I perceive I do. I want to be respected, not for how I look or what I have, but for who I am. I struggle with getting others to understand my personhood. How does one overcome the odds of being misjudged by others when the event is uncontrolled except in those rare instances when preparation, thought, and need are somehow revealed to those that share the same values at the same exact moment you do?

Until I began writing and reviewing this book, I thought humans had a seemingly vast capacity to bury their fears, sorrows, and unhappiness; however, I discovered that each of us has a breaking point, and all the negative emotions associated with events in one's life will need an outlet lest they overtake you and any number of tragic possibilities can manifest themselves. I chose to write.

With these thoughts, I begin my story.

Early Life

I often look back on my childhood and wonder how I ever survived it. Sound familiar? We each have a hard luck story to share, but what is amazing is that when unimaginable difficulties unfold in our lives, our coping mechanisms surface; and hopefully, our desire to overcome our struggles reveals our innate need to survive.

Birth is naturally where this story begins. Why? I was randomly placed by God with two well-intentioned, biological parents. So lucky! This is a good start—right? It was December 9, 1959.

As youngsters we think about our parents. I remember looking at myself in the mirror and then at my parents' features vs. mine. Were they really my parents? Many doubts entered my mind. I saw neither my mother's nose nor my father's. I thought perhaps I had been given to the wrong mom at the hospital. I think underneath was an overachiever's need to have the perfect parents, the perfect family. Mine seemed so far from the values that were already forming my psyche.

I wondered a lot about everything as a child; everything was a mystery and everything was new. I think I had a normal childhood up to about the age of seven. I was born. At some point I believed I had deciphered my first breaths of life. I was having difficulty breathing and gave up trying and blacked out but then awoke somehow and was breathing easier, and being.

My birth memory suddenly transforms and as the new one takes shape, I see myself now standing at the back door of an old farmhouse of sorts, chilled to the bone from the frigid winter air, banging at the door. Mom locks the door, ordering me to play in the abundant snow. I didn't want to go out, but my sisters embraced the opportunity with excitement. As soon as we entered the outdoors, they ran off to play, but I remained at the back door, knocking and knocking to be let back in. I believe I was outdoors for over an hour, deliberating what I should do alone in the cold and persistently knocking at the door to be let back in. Mom came to open the door just as my sisters returned from their excursion. They were quite excited. They found a leprechaun. Faith yelled, "Genevieve caught one. Look at what she got." Genevieve is my junior by one year, Faith my senior by same. I couldn't believe it. If I had gone along with them and not stubbornly stayed behind to beg reentry into the house, I could have shared their wondrous adventure.

Years later we bantered about whether or not leprechauns really existed. Genevieve and Faith, having witnessed the spectacle of this event, were adamant that they did in fact exist. Remembering my disappointment that I was not able to share the enthusiasm of their discovery and subsequent belief, I challenged their assertion. The frigid air kept me from venturing out. My sisters' speed and seeming need to leave me behind kept me from following after them. My mother's need to be alone left me out in the cold.

I have a few other memories as a child of two, three, and four. One was a family picnic. Mom and Dad decided to have a picnic one day. Dad set up a horseshoe game near the house. All of my then siblings wanted to play. At the time my siblings were Bonniemarie, the oldest; Sammy, the second (named after my father); Faith, the third oldest; and Genevieve, the youngest. We all seemed to spontaneously gather around the stake. I'm sure somehow my older siblings were directed or directed themselves there, along with my younger sister and me. They liked being bosses. My brother seemed to understand the game and said, "I want to go first." So...I think he did. I seemed to be learning the game as we played. I did not know how the game was played, but it soon became clear that you needed to throw the horseshoe toward the stake. If you got it on the stake, you won. It was finally my turn. I could not get it anywhere near the stake. The horseshoe was so heavy. As each turn throwing the heavy hunk of iron showcased my inability to overcome my handicap, I increasingly felt inadequate and envious of my siblings' triumphs.

All of a sudden a loud noise split the air and everyone looked away. I had not heard the noise, but I noticed they were all looking away. I seized the opportunity, scurrying forward, picking up the horseshoe, and putting it on the stake. I was not quite back to my spot when my brother turned and saw my movements. I started to shout, "I did it, I won," but my brother countered, "Amzy cheated." The accusation that I was a cheater made me upset because I knew even at age three or thereabouts that it was not a good one, and I ran off crying. I was embarrassed because I felt like a failure, but not because I couldn't ring the horseshoe. I don't remember how long I cried. The game disbanded as did my siblings. They didn't seem mad at me, just sorry.

My next memory is pushing a red tricycle up a hill in our front yard. The Brecksville home was right next to an elementary school, and there was a slight hill leading from our front yard up to the adjacent driveway which serviced the school. I decided to ride my tricycle on the pavement because it would be easy, smooth, and fun. It was difficult pushing the bike up the hill. I kept trying and trying and trying. I remember thinking, "I need to push with all my might." I figured out through trial and error how to hold and push the bike so it would not fall over as I elevated it up the soft, grassy slope. So with all my might and knowledge, I pushed. I made it!

Two interesting and funny things happened after this that helped me enjoy my success so much more. One was that my mom had observed me the entire time. She later told me that. "Amzy," she said, "I saw you pushing your bike up the hill today. You never gave up. Good for you." She was so happy for me and my success. Her words resonated with me and have stayed with me to this day. That afternoon Bonniemarie came home from the school. She must have been in second or third grade—she was born in 1956, three years my senior. She said, "Mommm. Mommm." "What, Bonniemarie?" my mother asked. She responded, "I was so embarrassed today. My sisters were in their slips riding their bikes in the playground. All my classmates and my teacher were laughing. I was so embarrassed. Please don't let them do that again!" As far as I know, we avoided her window from then on, and we all were able to look back and see both humor and charm in those innocent moments.

I'm now climbing around a basement bookcase, enjoying the triumph of having made it to the top, looking around, and feeling joy as I watch my siblings doing insane variations of climbing on and jumping off. I may have actually been younger at this house. I don't think so however. This house was in Parma or Parma Heights, Ohio (less than an hour away from the Brecksville farmhouse). It was a nice brick house. I remember many things from this house, all of them good memories. Perhaps one or two I did not understand; but all of them were good, good memories.

We had a backyard that was small and not private. My father seemed intent on making it private. We had moved from a rural setting to this suburban neighborhood. I now realize what a change it must have been for my parents. I loved it. The neighborhood had lots of other kids, and I couldn't wait to play with them and discover what they were like. I remember a young girl down the street. She had everything: a bigger house, nicely furnished, and a play set in the backyard. My father had succeeded at privatizing ours. He purchased redwood fencing which he arranged side by side around the backyard. Each fence was about five feet high and eight to ten feet wide. I think the neighbor behind us complained. I remember my father telling him he wasn't going to remove the fencing; he did not seem very friendly toward the man. I don't remember too much more about that.

My older sisters liked to venture over to the house that abutted my new friend's house. Schmidt was the surname. Both of my sisters seemed to like Matt Schmidt. The Schmidts had a big house, with a greenhouse in the backyard. Bonniemarie and Faith (and perhaps Sammy) would go there, but I never followed. I was always content to stop and visit my friend or her play set. I think at some point, though, I was told by my mom that I could not play on the set unless I was with a member of her family. I was a little confused and sad and thought, "What am I going to do instead? What is wrong with this?" The answer never came. "Just do what I told you," was the stock response.

I have a really cool memory from this neighborhood. Grandma, my father's mother (whom I shall refer to as Grandma Romauch), had come to watch us one day. She took Genevieve and me for a walk. Down the street from our home was a pond. On this day swans were there, and for the first time in my life, I saw these beautiful birds, floating gracefully over the water. My memory recaptures this moment, I am certain, because of the wonder I felt when I witnessed the solitude of these magnanimous birds in my mind and soul simultaneously as my eyes followed their majestic movements of white, fluffy perfection in S-shaped variations of form floating seemingly without overt means as they transformed the water into soft ripples of the reflected shimmery sky. Observing their alluring movements in the picturesque pond created a sudden urge in me to dive right in and join them.

Later that day or a few days later when we brought up the event, a family discussion of sorts ensued. As usual a real-world spin was placed on the adventure, which served to cloud my judgment of swans. Swans, I was informed, are very dangerous birds. You don't want to be on or in the water near them. Swans overturned a man's boat and he drowned. It was such a shocking story and I remember feeling sad for the man and, thereafter, less entranced with swans. This carries forward to this day. I love seeing them, but I don't linger. I think it is my way of coping with the fact that nature in all of its overt grandeur can be brutal.

The Lakewood House

The next two years of my life were also happy ones. We moved again, to a house in Lakewood. We all loved this house. I enjoyed many milestones here. In many ways I wish the move after this one never happened.

I loved the Lakewood house and every memory of it and our lives there. Isabelle would join us while we lived here and I was ready for kindergarten. The falls were gorgeous in Lakewood, and I do hope still are. Buckeyes, oaks, and maples littered the landscape. The leaves fell and we played in freshly mounted piles of assorted fallen foliage, wind swept into our backyard and then raked into the highest possible mountain of fall color Mom could arrange for us while we were away at school—or in my case, while I napped. Then during lunch Mom said, "If you finish your sandwich, you can go out and jump in the leaves." I was at a disadvantage. I arrived at the table after my brother and sisters' luncheon was well underway and they almost seemed finished so Mom's motivational prompt to finish just made them eat that much faster. I was tired, and as I took my first bite of food, I looked out back and noticed the enticing pile of wonder. I became motivated to stuff the sandwich down but it tasted terrible. I think it was bologna. As I began eating, my sisters and brother were finishing up. Even Genevieve finished before me. As I sat and ate as fast as I possibly could, I watched the pile of leaves become more and more diminished in height as each sibling joined in the pouncing and throwing of the leaves up around themselves. By the time I got out there, there was no pile left for me to jump into. I remember thinking, "The next time I am going to get to the leaves first." A next time did arrive and I think I managed to get a little time in with the small pile before every leaf was scattered; but I lost interest in leaf play—it didn't seem all that fun after all.

We got a dog! It was a beagle. It was so cute. I remember Mom and Dad making up a name for her, a girl dog. It had long, floppy ears and soft fur, and it shook with either excitement or fear. I remember it liked hanging around the wall vent where the heat came out. We all liked sitting there in the winter. I remember sitting there and petting Sheila a long, long time. As with everything, I had to share time with Sheila, but I could pet her when my siblings were at school. This was good. I don't remember why, but we couldn't keep Sheila. I think my parents decided that we couldn't afford the dog food and vet bills. So one day Dad took Sheila away. I don't know if he gave her back or what he did. Somehow I understood the importance of what they did. They did something for us. It was a tough decision. I missed Sheila for awhile, but something new always waited around each corner. So…I moved on.

We had new neighbors. The Savages! Mom announced that they had a girl my age. I was soooo happy! Wow…at last someone I could play with just for me. Well…why do we do that to ourselves? Why do we automatically assume something is just for us? I discovered over time that I also needed to share Maria with my sisters. But she was mostly my friend. She was definitely my friend first. We ran together, walked to school together, ate together, laughed together, and rode bikes together. At Halloween, I remember Maria handing out candy to me and smiling. I got mad at her once, only once. (I'll tell that story shortly.)

When they got a big swimming pool in their backyard, we were invited over. My name was always included in the invitation. Oh gosh, how happy I was! I think God gives us happy moments in our lives so we can stay sane in the future when things get tough. But I was happy then. I remember the time my sister Faith decided that Maria was going to be her friend. Genevieve was there to back her up. This made me upset. I remember following them to their side door (I don't know why, but everyone always knocked on a neighbor's side door when we wanted a friend to come out and play). I was behind them as they knocked. Maria and her mom answered the door. Faith said, "Can Maria come out and play with me?" They seemed a little confused because Genevieve and I were also there. It was weird. Maria's mom said, "It's okay, Maria. Who do you want to play with?' Maria said, "Faith." As she looked then to me and quickly then to Genevieve, she added, "And Genevieve." Beginning that moment and for

THE LAKEWOOD HOUSE

the next several months, my friendship with Maria was put on hold. She only answered a call to play with Faith and Genevieve. I was left out. I finally gave up trying to be part of the trio and went off and played alone yet again in my life. But it did not last forever. Somehow Maria decided to ask me to play again; she came to our house—in itself an unusual act—knocked on the door and asked to play with me. Wow...I was so, so happy.

I remember all the neighbors that had kids, whether the kids were my age or not. The Fromskirts and the Kashees lived right next to each other. Peggy Fromskirt was my age and we sat next to each other in kindergarten. Patrick Kashee was my age and I remember when I turned six years old going to his house with my mom. His mom said, "Patrick, don't you have something for Amzy?" He said, "Oh, can you help me get it down?" as he tried to reach up on top of a cabinet to get something that was way out of reach. His mom retrieved something and gave it to him, and he in turn gave it to me. I remember the feeling I had when he handed it to me. I think this was the first time I really loved a boy. He made me feel so good to have made *me* a birthday card. I had no idea he even thought about me. We hung out a lot off and on after that. I always liked Patrick.

My younger sister, Isabelle, made a strong friendship with his younger sister, Helen. Years later my mother, Genevieve, Isabelle and I went to visit the Kashees at their home in Amish country. They had decided to move out of the city. They thought it would be better, more affordable, and in keeping with the values they wanted for their kids.

Parents would be amazed if they knew how much we listened and perhaps did not fully understand, but remembered and eventually made sense of ourselves. I think listening was good. Did parents want us to listen to learn or did they selfishly only want their time? I never quite figured that out. I think it was more the latter because many times throughout my youth my parents said, "Children are meant to be seen and not heard."

Anyway...the boys were as excited to see us as we were to see them. I remember their reactions to Genevieve and me. They thought that Genevieve was me and I was Genevieve. We corrected them. But in my mind I knew why they had confused us. Genevieve was the beauty when we were young kids and I was the ugly duckling. It's strange how time can turn things around. Genevieve had changed, but she was still attractive. Her hair had been blonde and then changed to dark brown. She also was heavy in the hips. My hair had been a light brown and pretty much stayed that way. I was thinner than Genevieve, but she had been skinnier than me when we were younger. We flipped on these features so it was natural for the boys to mix us up based on their childhood memories. It was a grand visit just due to the fact that we saw them as young adults and the last time I had seen them was when I was six. One of the younger Kashee boys, Hughey, lost interest in us and rode off on a family horse. Patrick lingered and then insisted on taking Genevieve on a tour of the barn. Since I didn't seem invited, I went back to the house and ventured inside where Mom had gone with Isabelle and Helen. Mrs. Kashee had another infant. I was amazed that with fourteen kids she could have another baby. She spent some time with Mom and I ended up sitting in and listening to some of the Kashee family current events. Funny…I don't know anything about the Kashees today, but I bet Isabelle does. She loves her friends and keeps in touch with so many of them (some of mine included).

I was excited when it was time for me to walk to school with my sisters and brother. Our neighborhood parents were so cool. They all decided that on the first day of school we should all walk together and that the older kids were responsible for making sure that the younger ones got to school safely. I was afraid of going until I heard this rule and that I was specifically assigned to the older ones' care. I think Peggy Kashee was the first one assigned to me. I liked Peggy. I didn't talk to her, but I looked up to her because she was a take-charge kind of person. This made me think I would be safe and get to school just fine. Then a last-minute swap occurred and her sister Bridgette was in charge. I was slightly disappointed, but Bridgette seemed eager and confident, even though she was younger—I think thirteen.

So life was good. The first day was so exciting. We were so many we could have made up our own class. Let's see, let's say eight Kashees, four Romauches, three Savages, four Fromskirts, and the Satinos (a big family too). We were at least twenty-five that day. What a great memory. It was over a mile to the school. It seemed to take forever, and it was hard for me to keep up. I was so tired, but I was afraid they would leave me behind. I made it, but it was tough. I remember a couple remarks made about how slow I was. Now I look back and remember that it was because I was young, my legs were shorter and I was only six. Goodness.

As the days turned into weeks and the weeks into months, we lost our caravan, but different versions made the trek; and eventually, I met classmates along the way with whom I also shared the journey. I became acquainted with a boy and girl that almost looked like brother and sister. They always walked together and were very close friends. I think they eventually became so involved with just wanting to be together that they started avoiding me. I was a little confused by this and never quite figured it out. Looking back I can only imagine that they thought they didn't know me well enough to walk with me or invite me over for a visit.

I do recall one girl from my area, though, asking me over. It was amazing. I remember going to her house. She had been so excited that her mom said yes and my mom was okay with the visit. So one day I walked home with her. Almost as soon as we got there, she disappeared and I waited and waited for her just looking around at the things in their house. I was uncomfortable and somewhat embarrassed because I did not know why I had been left alone. Then she came back in the room and said that her mom wanted her to practice her harp. I asked if I could see it and she showed it to me. I asked her if she wanted me to stay and watch her practice or go home. So she went to ask her mom, and returned to report I should go home. I thought it was weird, but I left and started to walk home. Her house was further away from the school than ours, and I think I could not remember how to get home from her house. As I started leaving, I realized

I did not know the way, and I had to go back and ask them how to get home. I think her mom called mine and my mom came and picked me up. I was never invited back.

It surprised me when I met this girl again in college; we were in the same dormitory. She was very smart and helped me study calculus, and I really liked her, but we never became close friends. I don't know where she is today, but we both graduated in '82 from a private university in an eastern suburb of Cleveland, Ohio. Colleen, I think, was her name. I remember asking her if she had grown up in Lakewood and attended St. Clements, and she said she had. I asked her if she still played the harp. I asked her if she remembered me; she didn't. Life is weird. Something I could never forget, she had no memory of. It was such a coincidence that we both ended up at the same university. I think if I saw her today we would enjoy catching up, but in the end she wouldn't care to be my friend. Why is it that some people have a million friends and others find them hard to make—and even harder to keep? Why?

Just to fit this in, I need to finish off about our Lakewood friends and neighbors with a little silly story about Maria, as I said I would. We obviously were the same age. Maria moved in next door sometime after my year in the public school kindergarten class so I was very pleased to discover she and her brothers were going to attend the private school with me and my siblings. Maria and I ended up not having the same first grade teacher, but we romped to school together on occasion and still got quite excited when we saw each other in the hallways at school. Maybe we were in the same classroom together because I have a distinct memory of being lined up in the hallway one day and partnering with her in line. We needed to stand in two lines next to a partner and wait for our turn to go into the gym or through it, to leave for lunch. We would walk all the way home, have our lunch, then turn around and walk all the way back.

Looking back I can't believe how incredible that was. I don't know how long we did it, but I do recall some discussion by the adults about how difficult it was for us to return to school in a timely fashion. I think the tardy situation at some point got a little out of control. Anyway, Maria and I were somehow partnered together—this was extremely rare; and afterwards the teachers intentionally kept us apart. She said to me, "Amzy, open your mouth." I thought it a little odd, but having a trusting nature, I did. She quickly spit into it. I was so grossed out that I spit her spit out onto the floor and whatever expression came to mind spilled out with it. We were separated and I stayed away from her for I do not recall how long. Wouldn't that make you angry at a friend? Well…it did me, and to this day I think a little bile unexpectedly flows into my friendships to almost ruin or, in many cases, destroy them.

Another event from this time was when we all got bikes—all of us! Dad decided it was time that we all learn how to ride, though I don't know what triggered this sudden concern. So he took most of us kids on a shopping trip. We looked at bikes of all colors, sizes, and features, like bells and brakes and handle bars. Of course, being kids we all got an idea of what our favorite bike should be. I found out boys' and girls' bikes were different, the boys' bikes having a bar which extended across from the handlebar shaft to the seat shaft while the bar for a girl's bike was configured in a V-shape. I didn't get why at the time, and really it still seems something of a mystery. Anyway, Sammy and Bonniemarie got the biggest bikes. Faith's bike was a tad smaller. Genevieve and I got small, red ones with training wheels. Dad and Mom secretly brought the new bikes in and hid them in the detached garage in the rear of the lot. You could feel the energy surge out of my older siblings when we were collectively shown them. They seemed to learn to ride quickly. I don't remember specifics about who rode without falling down first. I have a vague memory of Dad teaching basic riding techniques to Bonniemarie, Sammy and Faith. Since Genevieve and I had training wheels, we just had to get used to being higher up on something that required a little more effort to balance than our former tricycles.

About a year later, Mom told the older kids to take us down the street to the parking lot, which served a vacant office complex, and teach us how to ride. I remember finally getting off respectably well because Peggy Kashee ran beside and then behind my bike and yelled, "Peddle as fast as you can, Amzy," and "You're doing fine," and "Amzy, you just rode six houses without my help!" She was good. That was all it took. I knew how to ride. Genevieve had similar training, and considering she was a year younger, it may have taken her an outing or two more, but she too learned how that summer.

We could go visit Grandma and Grandpa Romauch anytime we wanted. Their house was a mile north of ours, near Lake Erie. I was too young to walk there, but I do recall that Grandma walked to our house a couple of times to visit or babysit. I am sure it was babysit. Mom did not have a good relationship with Grandma, but I never heard her argue or fight with her. Mom would just seem uncomfortable. I could see it in her face and hear it in her voice as she conversed with Grandma. But Grandma came to help and I looked forward to spending time with her. She told stories about how her mom carried her over to America as a young child my age. Later in life she gave me a photograph of her taken at age four, my age at the time she first told me about immigrating. Grandma remembered she told me the story of how she, her mom, and her youngest brother (who was an infant) immigrated to America. I realized how thoughtful Grandma could be because the picture she gave me had been given to her by her mother, and she wanted me to have it. She picked me to tell the story to and to be the keeper of the family tree—only me, not any of my siblings.

About ten years ago, I researched the Ellis Island website and found their ship manifest. I keep it with the family tree Grandma gave to me for safekeeping during a visit I had with her in 1993. At this time Grandma and Grandpa lived in a retirement community in Hemet, California. I still have the picture, the family tree, and the manifest. Mom says to this day that Grandma was born in America. Perhaps she is correct, but my memory of what Grandma told me is different. Grandma told me she came to America through Ellis Island and apparently the records authenticate this. However, Grandpa was born in America, moved back to Yugoslavia, and then came to settle again in America. His name doesn't appear on any manifest because he didn't immigrate. Grandpa's family is a little bit of a mystery though because I couldn't locate a manifest for his father or his mother. Recently I learned during a visit to Ellis Island that many names were cut short or not understood correctly or written down incorrectly so the records are not always clear. As a result a relative may not be found even though they may have entered the States through this route.

Grandma always served us ginger ale when we visited. Grandma and Grandpa had a three-level house. They lived on the first floor and rented the second and upper floors to separate families. We visited my grandparents on holidays like Christmas and Easter. Grandma also wanted us to come over for Sunday dinners. I don't remember when she said we should do this, but I know we did for awhile and then for one reason or another the Sunday dinners stopped as a regular visit.

Grandma was a great cook. I remember once when she was babysitting us, she made strudel. She made the crust using an endless amount of dough that she industriously rolled and pulled and rolled and pulled to fit the size of our round dining table, which was about seventy-two inches. It was amazing! When the dough was ready, she went and got the apple mix and spread it out over the dough. Then she rolled the dough around the apples and cut it into strips to bake. You know how good something is when you make it the first time and it turns out perfectly? Well, that's how it was with this strudel. It was the best apple strudel I ever tasted. This event made me love anything apple my whole life, but I have never tasted better apple strudel than I did from that batch. Never.

Once Grandma brought up the subject of having studio pictures taken of Genevieve at Higbee's, a department store chain, and one of its fanciest locations was in the Terminal Tower in Cleveland, Ohio. When I was growing up, the terminal was the highest building in Cleveland and was considered a skyscraper. Grandma worked in the men's sock department. Can you imagine a whole department for men's socks? Well, when Grandma brought up the idea of the studio portrait session, I was standing right there with them. "Bonnie," she said, "I would like to take Genevieve for pictures at the Higbee's studio. I know the photographer and I told him about Genevieve and he would like to take her picture for me." (I really was a child to be seen and not heard and who apparently had no feelings.) I was hurt. Mom didn't even have to look at me. She immediately said, "It would be nice if Amzy and Genevieve had their pictures taken." Grandma quickly shot her a look and said, "Of course I would like to take both of them, but I will only do colored pictures of Genevieve." (Again, I was hurt because somehow I knew colored pictures were better because of Grandma's tone of voice.) So this was okay and they proceeded to make the date. It was so exciting. Mom picked out special clothes for us. Genevieve wore a sleeveless blue dress, and against her blonde hair and with touch-ups, the pictures were stunning. I was a little perplexed because Mom picked out a plaid dress with a white blouse for my pictures. Looking back I know it didn't matter what I wore because my pics were not going to be colored. I think I may even recall Grandma saying, "Just pick out something nice for Amzy to wear, and Bonnie, brush her hair." I have this portrait to this day and I am cute if I must say so myself. Yes, I must.

Going to the studio and the time spent with Grandma was memorable. She took us to lunch at the Silver Grill, and the food was nothing like I had ever tasted before. It was also the first time I saw Grandma working, for we went to meet her at the men's sock counter. It makes me laugh thinking about how quaint this was. Grandma was anything but quaint. Still in all, deep down I loved my grandma, even if she didn't think I was pretty. Somehow no matter how adults get along with each other, grandmas manage to find special ways to do things for their grandchildren. This makes them endearing, not perfect. I had many one-on-one experiences with Grandma growing up, and what I loved her for was the fact that she was there and she cared and even though she didn't always show good example or manners, somehow I always knew she loved me. She was definitely a lady who wore her opinion on her sleeve (trite, but true).

I recently told my memory of the Higbee's photography day to Mom. She remembered it quite well, but she disagreed with me about Grandma's reasons for wanting color pictures of Genevieve. She said, "Amzy, you were gorgeous. Grandma liked Genevieve because of how Genevieve always talked to her. She wanted a color picture of Genevieve because she had such a gregarious personality." I still wondered why a compliment would be seemingly given to one child in the presence of another. I was crushed now for a different reason and it reinforced my feelings of inadequacy in yet another way. I am a self-critical person and I don't know why. I wish I could be more generous with my own qualities and not get hung up on what others think about me. I find it hard to acknowledge another's good qualities because I am not always sure what my own are. I am so insecure. Why?

Some unusual neighbors lived on Elbur Avenue. We lived next to the nicest elderly lady you could imagine. Mrs. Blane I think her name was. She looked so old to me. If I recall correctly, she was in her nineties. She was thin and tall and walked with a youthfully graceful stature even though her upper back had a slight hump. Her house was alluring because the lawn was perfectly manicured and her flowers never seemed to stop blooming. She had bleeding hearts, honeysuckle and many others varieties of flowers that I cannot recall. She took my mother, sister, and me around her yard one day and pointed out which flowers not to touch. The bleeding hearts were off-limits because they were so difficult to cultivate. She was very proud that she was able to get them to grow. They were incredible and they really did look like bleeding hearts, but they were pink with streaks of red (I would have thought a heart was red, only red). I just wanted to squeeze and pop them because they were so plump. I loved the honeysuckle. It was my free-time hobby (along with my sister Faith and brother Sammy) to pick this flower and suck the nectar out of the bottom tip. It was like sucking on a soft, delicious straw. I was so disappointed I could never pick them again. I tried several times to sneak over and take one, but Mom always caught me. She seemed to know how tempting it was for me to do this and watched me like a hawk. I finally gave up this play activity, but spied Faith and Sammy on a few occasions succumbing to the honeysuckle's enticing aroma.

Another neighbor was always talking to himself. He looked like he was in his twenties or older. He incessantly talked to himself while walking down the street and often seemed to be carrying a large load of books. Everyone seemed to think he was okay, and I remember just accepting him for the way he was. He never spoke to me, and I would look at him as he passed. At first I said hello, but then I realized he never said hi back. He was just talking. After talking about it with Mom or someone, perhaps my sister, I made sure I didn't stare. I think I learned a street tactic at such a young age—if something isn't right, look past it like you don't even see it. So that's what I did.

The Joyces across the street had a girl or granddaughter with blonde hair that looked to be about my age. Blonde hair stands out. When I saw her the first time, I asked Mom if I could play with her. She seemed to want the same because she was staring at us (Genevieve and me) from across the street. Mom had a strict rule: Genevieve and I were not allowed to cross the street without an adult or an older sibling. So we had to get Mom to take us across and she did. After that, whenever we saw her, we would plead to go over and play. She was there to visit her grandpa who had a shaking problem with his hand. This is when I first learned that there was a disease that caused this. They said he was paralyzed this way. They meant that he could not help it. I remember them calling it by a long name that ended in "palsy." Today I realize the term was probably cerebral palsy. Anyway, he did not seem to shake too badly (mostly, his hands shook), and he seemed nice. But he did not talk too much.

Our neighbors, the Carolstons, lived the farthest away. They didn't visit too often. Anne Carolston was a year older than me. We visited together once or twice until Faith decided she was her age and her friend. Then every time I wanted to play with her, so did Faith. Finally, it was decided that Anne was too old for me, but it was okay for me to hang out with her younger brother who was my age. One time we got together and walked up toward our house. Somehow—I don't remember how this happened—we both wanted to know what our butts looked like. I may have dared him to pull down his pants first and he did! So then I had to. We each took turns quickly pulling our pants down and back up, down and back up… It was so funny, we started laughing and didn't stop as we continued on with each of at least six or seven turns—I was exhausted from laughing so hard. As there was nothing else to do, I said I wanted to go home. So I said goodbye, and went inside. I don't think he wanted me to go, but there was nothing else to do. I think I thought maybe something was wrong with what we did. It's one of those growing up memories you don't typically tell anyone about. I guess they may think you're weird. I look back and think, "I was normal." Curious is normal, right?

I think I've hit the highlights about unusual neighbors, but many other experiences storm into my mind from the little time we lived in our Elbur home. I remember going to a birthday party of the young girl I played with when we lived in Parma Heights. Mom came into our bedroom one Saturday morning. Genevieve and I were still sleeping, my older sisters long gone, and when she woke us, she announced, "Amzy, you and Genevieve are invited to… (I can't remember her name) …birthday party. The party starts at one p.m. so I need you both to get dressed in something nice. Genevieve, here is something for you to wear. Amzy, what do you want to wear?" I looked in the closet, which was a mess, and couldn't find anything as nice as Genevieve's outfit. I think Mom suggested I wear a white blouse and skirt. If I could only find the blouse…I sifted through the clothes on the closet floor. Genevieve came over. We both checked, and as she moved something, I noticed it. "Here it is." Mom came in and took it. She said she would iron it and bring it back. When she returned with it neatly pressed, I retrieved it from her and put it on as she helped Genevieve dress. I asked, "Mom, what are we going to eat for breakfast?" She said we would eat at the party and not to worry about it.

We arrived and it was so strange; we walked into the backyard just like I used to when we lived down the street. The play set was empty, and I wished I could play on it even though I knew the birthday party was underway. Mom realized that she would need to go around to the front of the house to get in. As she rounded the corner carrying Genevieve on her hip, she glanced back at me and told me to stay off the play set.

I waited forever, and I was just about to sit on one of the swings when the back patio door opened and I was asked to come in. The house was so nice inside. They had a plaid wall-to-wall carpet. I followed my mom upstairs where all these kids were seated around the dining room table and I soon figured out they already ate. I was just in time to join in singing 'Happy Birthday'. "Amzy, would you like a piece of cake?" I enthusiastically replied, "Yes. Is there anything else to eat?" Mom piped in, "No, Amzy, just cake."

The birthday girl opened our gift which was a book with pop-outs. When Mom had shown Genevieve and me what our gift was, I had wanted to open it and look at every page, but Mom said, "No Amzy, wait until the birthday girl opens it." Well, the book was a big hit so I had to wait and wait for it to make the rounds before I could look at it. When I finally got it, I quickly became entranced with each page, but I barely began, when Mom said, "Time to go. Amzy, let's go." I couldn't believe it. I had to close the book and follow her out. This was what a birthday party is like? I did not like it at all. The only thing that was good about it was that the birthday girl liked our gift, as did all the other kids. One more thing I liked about that party was that it was the first one I ever went to for a friend. It would be a really long time before the next one.

I am remembering how my dad was as a person. He died from a stroke. He had high blood pressure and some type of chemical imbalance that caused three or four heart attacks, which he finally got under control until the stroke. He died at the age of fifty-three. He was a butcher by trade, and so many big things happened in our lives because of his somewhat fearless demeanor and his way of reacting to people by arguing with them. He would raise his voice and state his thoughts and usually this was somewhat unexpected. I was too young to understand his triggers or recognize them as such. So he seemed a little random and short-tempered to me. Perhaps this is how others viewed him too.

I see similar personality traits in me at times—the female version of my father—when I lash out verbally at my children for some wrong they have committed in my eyes, which in the grand scheme of things may not be important. I worry a lot more than the average person but perhaps not more than the average mom. So if my son comes home from school with a bad grade, I am on it. I need to know why, I need to know when, and I need to know it will never happen again. That's it. I am on it and will not relent. Well...in reality, this does not always work that great. Abraham will get upset; he may even become apologetic and cry that I am being too hard on him. I listen to his concerns and soon (with the help of Dad) dole out a punishment that fits the crime. This approach toward parenting has its own pitfalls, but somehow I believe it is better because it encompasses the situation and the person. It gives our kids a chance to explain themselves. It is our job as parents to make sure our kids don't have the same problems we had from being hit or strapped for talking back or lying about something rather than discovering the underlying problem and addressing the issue head-on and problem-solving it with them. Once all the emotions have run their course, the situation should improve and hopefully it is a win-win for everyone with a lesson learned.

I think part of the problem is that what our parents corrected us for when we were growing up was viewed as disciplinary; our parenting methods today extend beyond this to factor in the coping strategies that are still developing in a young person. So even though my spouse and I usually employ corrective measures as a direct result of an undesirable outcome, and kids don't usually realize the need for corrective action—just like when I was growing up—they can then come to terms with why their actions were wrong and how they can hurt themselves and/or others.

We try to listen to them and what they're going through; and we challenge their behaviors and tell them they can do better. I get so much more satisfaction out of knowing my kids respect me because I listen to them rather than coming away with fear and resentment that they possibly could bury somewhere inside of them as I did. If I happened to do the right thing, it may have been because I learned from listening to the story of a sibling or a friend and not because my parents taught me a life lesson by hitting me. Ultimately it took me longer to create a strong value system because getting hit made me fearful which interfered with my ability to understand what I did wrong. I couldn't ask questions to understand better because I possibly would get spanked again. At times this query would earn me the right to return to my room to think more about what I did wrong.

With my kids, when I choose the wrong behavior to correct or analyze, my reaction is to over-apologize. This is my way of making up not only for over-reacting but for trying to seek forgiveness from them because my siblings and I never felt forgiven. We may have said we were sorry, and most of the time we deeply were. But something else, which never surfaced, was in my mind: We were sorry because we simply wanted our parents to be nice and love us again. The lesson learned was secondary. Our parents didn't know it, but they slowly turned us into emotional cripples.

Father (and Mother at times) believed in corporal punishment for what he viewed as severely bad behavior, which I think was something we were supposed to know was wrong, but did anyway. We would all be lined up in a room, like the dining room—for some reason this room springs to mind as memorable. My father would proceed to interrogate us to discover the main culprit(s). It was usually a she said, he said kind of thing, so my father found it difficult to determine the guilty party. I would stand by hoping Dad wouldn't turn to me and somehow include me in what seemed to be a trivial incident. Sometimes my younger siblings and I were excused because we were younger and the older ones should have set a better example. This served to confuse me somehow, and then I would feel sorry for my older sisters and brother. I suppose I felt these attacks on us were not necessary because I didn't really understand what anyone did that was wrong. Most of the sibling arguments were power plays for one to gain the right to something, whether it was some kind of snack from the fridge or who should have the last piece of blank paper to complete a homework assignment.

It really was all so hazy then, as now, but I believe many of my father's actions, like my own misjudgments, were stress-related. He was not always thinking clearly about the purpose of punishments during these times. When this happened we siblings dwelled on the pain and embarrassment of Dad's punishment rather than a constructive examination of what went wrong and how it could have been handled better. This was compounded by the fact that his approach was to interrogate, decide who was guilty, and hopefully dismiss the uninvolved parties (thank God, because he could just as easily have punished all of us if he wished). Then the guilty parties were subjected to a strapping and usually made to stand in place and think about what they did wrong. This was the most severe of punishments. How they could have handled things better was never discussed.

Dad employed more lenient forms of punishment. I recall once that he did not like how Faith and Sammy were kneeling in church. When we got home, they were made to kneel in front of the fireplace for three hours, just the way they should have in church. I was once given this punishment as well, but Mom saw to it that I could get up much sooner, after Dad had to leave to go somewhere.

He was fond of family outings that required short travel time and no admission fees, like clam bakes and visits to Slovenian picnics. I loved his energy, but it also scared me. He was a dichotomy of someone who loved life, loved his family, but was self-possessed and closed-minded.

It may be somewhat surprising for me to relay that I have some touching memories of my father. Somehow as bad as he could be toward us, he could also be kind. It was clear he cared for us because he never abandoned us even when it seemed like he should have. Up until about two years ago, I had no pictures of him. I acquired two great snapshots during a summer family reunion when we were gathered around looking at my uncle's family album, which contained several pictures that reminded me of some of the good and somewhat funny things that I found endearing about Dad.

As I look at the photos, I suddenly feel the inner spirit of my dad breaking out of the boundaries of the paper, sending me visual messages that relate to some pain I am currently experiencing with personal friendships. I selected these photos as a keepsake of my dad, but viewing them together has given me a new perspective—the small moments can help bring us through the tough times. These remembrances are not only beckoning me back, they are my dad looking back at me as though to remind me that success and failure are not the most important things in life. It's the brief moments in which we share a little bit of who we are—or in the case of Dad, who we were—that gives meaning and true value to our lives. This is a lot to digest, so let me break it down.

In one picture Dad has a towel around his head because he, like me, suffered from bad migraines. Dad looks silly and that's the point. He needed that towel on his head to relieve his pain, but in the process of healing, he had to look silly. We all thought him odd, but we all knew that Dad needed to be left alone to repair and rest when that towel was there. Dad was human, and we knew him to be just as vulnerable to pain as we were. The fact that Dad laughed when his picture was taken means he had a sense of humor too. Score one for him.

Another picture shows Dad holding a life preserver. The instant I took a closer look at the photograph, I knew Dad was drawing me in for a purpose. My first reaction to this picture was that it was a reminder of a time when our parents took us on a canoe trip. We went on a couple of them, and the first adventure was sixteen to twenty miles on a pretty brisk waterway. It was scary, exhilarating, and fun: Scary because I was a young girl in a canoe in water and afraid I could drown if the canoe tipped over; exhilarating because it gave me a good dose of excitement that, as the day wore on, turned into an appreciation of the fact that my parents really loved us kids to spend a whole day just having fun; and fun because we splashed, we swam, we ate on the bank, we worried about our picnic and our food, and we all did it together for a whole day! How much better does it get?

I don't believe in ghosts, but I do in spirits. They speak to us somehow, and for this reason society has given them a magical, mystical existence where people believe they actually see them (but perhaps—they simply need to.) An image I need to formulate from this picture is contained in the life preserver Dad is holding. It is a symbol telling me that life is so much more than all of the hype everyone attaches to worldly success. Like the preserver bobbing on top of water, recognizable for what it is, a lifesaving device, real character stands out and has more value when it is discovered and sustained through the quality of our relationships (and not at all by the quantity of them). My dad is throwing me a life preserver because I feel I need it. I feel like I am drowning (the reasons for which shall be shared later). He is there to remind me that life is more than how others define success, even more than how "perfect me" defines it. I just need to figure out what that is. Success may be part of having good, healthy relationships with others. But I need to forgive myself when those friendships don't work out. It is not always the other guy's fault or my own. Failure in friendships just happens even if I am trying to do everything I can to save or create them. There he is looking out at me, reminding me there is more to life than money or success or sometimes friendships. Even when we fail, it's what we do with that failure that allows us to stay afloat. "Here, Dad, I'm out for the pass. I hope I've got it." In this picture, Dad is holding the life preserver to give to one of us kids before we get in the boat. I can place myself in the picture and feel the warmth of the sun, the exciting anticipation of getting into the canoe and embarking on our watery fun-filled trip, and the goodness of the inner personhood of my Dad. It's amazing how a picture can do this, isn't it? I prefer to remember Dad this way.

As an adult only one year away from the same age Dad was when he passed away, I am happy we are seemingly drawing life from each other in a way that was never possible when he was alive. These are helpful, wholesome insights, free of pain and full of love. It's amazing that even though we suffered so much pain in our lives, it now seems that the essence of what was good survived. This picture is one of Dad taken at some point during the canoe trip. He shared his life, his time, and his livelihood with us while he could. He shared his personhood as the son of a second-generation immigrant from Slovenia, whose life growing up was not easy. He made sure we spent time with family and was proud of us, even though it didn't always seem that way. He was too quick with physical punishments, but it was well intentioned and probably a carbon copy of how he had been raised.

Another fine point about Dad that I need to include is that he was an artist. He had phenomenal color, shape, and texture perceptions, which he could capture on canvas and in mosaic forms. I said he was a dichotomy in temperament, but he was as well in intellect. He was a gifted artisan who was stuck in a butcher's persona. How frustrated he must have been. I realize, at this precise moment, my father and I metaphorically coexist. I wish I could talk with him about what we share in common. I wonder, if Dad were alive, would I?

A physical description of Dad seems appropriate. He stood six feet, two inches tall, had dark hair, and blue eyes with perfect vision. As a child growing up, I never saw him as handsome, just as Dad. Mom fell in love with his appearance. She said, "All my friends heads turned when I walked in the room with Dad." Unfortunately I misinterpreted Mom's emphasis on Dad's good looks to mean that appearances are important. It took years for me to learn that looks aren't everything—my own and those of others, especially guys.

Over the years I began to grapple with the reason looks were the focal point attracting me to boys and them to me, and why they would abandon me. I started to try and figure out what was wrong with this value. I thought, "Hmmm, Mom and Dad were born in the mid-thirties, which meant they were young adults in the late forties, early fifties. Greased hair, poodle skirts, and cashmere sweaters became the preppy look for both sexes during my late teens and lasted quite some time. The male stereotype of tall, dark, and handsome, however, was a standard that transcended my parents' generation." I remember Dad once saying, "I loved your mother's butt." Okay, this is weird, but they each clearly were attracted to physical traits in the other, so much so that they said "they fell in love" with them. In the back of my mind I somehow stored that fact; they didn't fall in love with the inner person, but with the appearance of the other. This may have helped me eventually realize that appearances aren't everything. But the romance of being with the ideal mate in every way was enticing, misguiding, and shattering. It's good I waited to marry in spite of myself.

Denison—Day One

Moving on, unfortunately, I need to now describe the most horrific of moves, one almost surpassed by a recent one in my adult life but not quite, thank God. I do hope it stays that way. One fall day shortly after I started second grade, my siblings and I were told we would wake up the next morning and get dressed as always, but we would be going to a new school; and after school we would be coming home to a new house. I remember my reaction as one of surprise and a little wonder mixed with fear. After we were all dressed and ready to go, we had to pile into the car. The house was full of boxes and on the verge of emptiness. Mom and Dad drove us to a restaurant that seemed very far away. We went in and ordered breakfast. Everyone wanted pancakes, but when they came and we started eating them, they didn't taste too great. Mom said that the first person to finish the pancakes could have a donut. This time I won. It's interesting how everything we needed to race for involved eating food. Mom really had a way of motivating us to eat.

Afterward we all went out to the car. It was starting to get lighter out. We then drove to our new school. I remember some things but ever so vaguely. I remember learning about how Mom and Dad were married in the church next to the school and driving around the streets which surrounded the area, as though we were being given a tour by a real estate agent.

As part of the tour, Dad drove into and briefly around the parking lot that serviced the school as well as the church. Then he said, "Bonnie, do you know where the office is?" Mom guessed it was in the larger of the two school buildings. Mom was right—the office was in the bigger of the two school buildings, the one that had nice gold bricks. I hoped my classroom would be there. I watched my sisters and brother get sent away one by one by the principal who methodically discovered ages, grades, and grade levels in order to place each of us in the right classroom. Our group dwindled, starting with the oldest and moving down in age. My sister Genevieve and I were last. I thought since I was older than she, they would take me away next, but they didn't: I was last. Genevieve took a young lady's hand and then the principal turned to Dad and Mom and said, "Our tuition is $25 a month per student." Once their conversation turned in a direction that did not concern me, I began ignoring them and looking around the office.

It seemed as though I had to wait forever for them to finish their discussions. Mom then looked over at me as did the principal. It was finally my turn. "I think she can go with Sister Bernadette." So off we went to my new class and to meet my new teacher. I think my parents and the principal agreed to $100 per child for tuition, which was a significant savings. I am sure the amount had to be renegotiated again and again over the years to come.

My new class was nothing that I ever could have imagined. It was in the smaller of the two buildings, so we needed to walk across the huge parking lot, which I would soon discover, also served as the playground. From a distance I saw my sister just reach an entry door into the opposite side of the complex where I was being taken. I had hoped I could discover where her classroom was. I was taken up a flight of stairs; the person taking me left me at the door and strode in to tell my new teacher I was there. They spoke to each other quietly for a few moments and then my guide left me to enter on my own.

I remember walking in and standing in front of what seemed like a room full of at least fifty kids. I don't really know how big it was, but it sure seemed like more kids than in the class I had at St. Clements. As I stood facing the class, I glanced over at a nun wearing a long, black habit and sitting behind a desk near the opposite corner from the door. She looked up acknowledging me. My guide came back, walking by me as she left, and I stood alone and quite nervous. "Class, we have a new student," the nun said. "Her name is Amzy Romauch. I am Sister Bernadette, Amzy. Now please go sit…" she trailed off, "…there, in the second row in the second-to-last seat." I hesitated for a moment, looking at this ancient woman in a black habit.

This was the first time I had a nun as a teacher, so her appearance took me off guard. She reminded me of the witch from *Snow White and the Seven Dwarves*. I quickly realized I had to do as she instructed, so off I went to sit down. Then she continued with her lessons and I tried to understand what she was teaching. I think I arrived in the middle or end of a geography lesson.

Someone tapped me on the shoulder from behind. I turned around and saw that the girl behind me wished to talk. As soon as I turned, Sister Bernadette said, "Oh, the new girl is so good and is such a good listener." Well, as I realized she was talking about me, I wondered why she would say this when it was obvious she had seen me turning around and probably doing the opposite of what she wanted. This went on for several days. Then one day she put me in the time-out seat, which was not desirable. I was so upset and embarrassed and I remember crying. This was devastating because it wasn't me that had caused the problem, it was Priscilla. I can't believe I still remember her name. She had thick, brown poofy hair. She was actually pretty dumb, I thought, because she talked instead of listening quietly to learn.

When I got home that day, I told my mom what had happened. She came in the next day to talk to Sister Bernadette. Shortly after that my seat was changed, along with the seats of several other students. I never again had this problem, and I was so relieved to return to peace and quiet.

I need to back up a little and describe what happened at the end of the first day and my impressions of the new house. Mom came and picked us up. This would be one of the few times she drove us home. As she drove, she pointed out how we would walk to and from school. I looked at the new streets as we went. The area was different: more traffic and traffic lights, store fronts, and two funeral homes—not just houses and trees. Then we turned into the driveway. I don't remember what I thought, but I guess I was curious more about how our new house looked inside. Somehow I didn't like it, probably because it was strange. It had a lot of dark wood everywhere. The kitchen had bright yellow tile, and cabinets filled one of the walls. The sink had a small countertop on each side, and Mom figured out that the counter top on the right was actually the lid of a dishwasher. She seemed quite happy until she and Dad discovered later that it didn't work.

We wandered upstairs to see the rest of the house. As we walked by each room and peered inside, Mom satisfied our curiosity about which bedroom would belong to whom. She and Dad had the largest bedroom. I loved their room. It had a huge closet. The other rooms were nice too. I liked the room across from my parents, but I would never sleep in that room. I don't remember, but I think Isabelle went in this room. Genevieve and I were assigned the room near the top of the stairs. It was okay. I didn't like it as well because it had a linoleum floor—not carpeting like Isabelle's. Mom directed us toward a staircase that took us up another level. At the top was a small hallway with a bathroom in the center and bedrooms on opposite sides. Mom gave Sammy the back bedroom, and Bonniemarie and Faith the room in front, which appeared to be larger. "All you girls may be up here someday," Mom said. This eventually did happen, but I don't recall what triggered the change. I thought it would be cool to be in a place where it was just "the girls."

To quickly explain, the house faced south on an avenue with ongoing automobile and truck traffic. Across the street was a bricked strip of businesses, including a bar—the Double A bar to be exact—a Laundromat and perhaps something else which I do not recall. Some homes extended along the avenue on either side of the business strip. Directly across, adjacent to the brick business strip, was a street, which I later would walk up and down many, many times just for something to do or for exercise.

I think we discussed dinner, and we were whisked off to Grandma's, Mom's mom (whom I shall refer to as Grandma Braun), to return much later. Mom scrambled around trying to find sheets and bedding to prepare the beds. Thinking back I realize how much work she had to do for us then. She managed to find sheets for all the beds, and we all were fast asleep in a wink. It had been a big day and we were obviously all pooped.

Denison—Dad's Decline

Life in the new house was very different. We didn't have a caravan of neighbors to escort us to school on the first real day because this wasn't the first day of school. We had moved and even though it was for us, it really wasn't. We partnered together, brother and sisters, and made our way to our new school, traveling the route Mom had mapped out for us the day before. School seemed closer to home than our last house. My oldest sister, Bonniemarie, talked as we walked, pointing out that our walk to school was much, much shorter and insisted it would only take us fifteen minutes to walk it each day, rather than our previous forty-five-minute walk. It was shorter but not as pretty. We became well acquainted with this bland walk. Genevieve and I were enticed by Faith to try a new route. She said she found a shortcut, which actually ended up being longer. Eventually I grew tired of the longer route and announced that I was going to return to the old one. Genevieve seemed to mull this over, and although at first she wanted to continue with the newer route, she decided to bag it and side with me, which rarely happened. Genevieve and Faith chummed up together in a way that left me out. I think it started on Maria Savage's doorstep and would continue to influence our trio in the future more often than I would have liked—this situation the exception. It was odd though, and perhaps Genevieve knew this, but it made me feel good when she went my way or agreed with me on something. It was like she knew I needed to be right every once in awhile, but also that I craved the companionship.

When I looked out the front of our house, I saw a bar across the street, not the Joyces with the dad or grandpa with shaky hands. We would find making new friends different in this neighborhood, which consisted of Catholic school kids and public school kids. The latter seemed to worry my parents, but we made friends with the neighbors eventually. Even when we did, we debated about who was okay and who wasn't. What was okay? I wondered. I walked back and forth from school, back and forth, back and forth. Eventually I made many friends, most of them from school. One of these friends ended up becoming my best friend, but that changed. I'll go into this more later.

We lived in the Denison house from the time I was in second grade until I graduated from eighth. Many bad things happened here and, unfortunately, I need to recount them.

My father lost his business. I can't remember exactly how old I was when this happened—perhaps nine or ten—but I knew it was a bad thing. I remember Dad telling Mom he was taking a cashier job in the local Open Pantry only three houses down on the corner. It had been exciting watching it get built, and for a while we wondered what it was going to be. Then a neighbor or family member told us it was going to be a mini food mart. The store went up on a former gas station site. One of the outer walls from that station was used as a wall for the new store. I thought that was very interesting. Anyway, Dad asked for a job, and they took him. Then he talked to Mom about her working and she was okay with it, especially since she had wanted to go back to work on several other occasions but Dad had said no. Now everything was different. So the management, a married couple, hired Mom too. A short time later Dad was fired. I think he was not nice to a customer and they said he was too short-tempered. He wanted to run everything his way and was hard to work with. I remember wondering why Dad was like this, especially when he knew we needed the money.

To back up a little, Dad was a good man, but something changed him. He owned and operated a successful grocery store which featured a butcher counter of freshly cut meats he prepared and sold daily. Mom would occasionally help out in his store. It was on a main avenue in or near Lakewood, but I am not sure where. I know it was a busy area and he had established himself as a good butcher. He changed store locations thinking that it would be more profitable, but the opposite happened. I remember him coming home one day and telling Mom he lost his lease and there was nothing he could do. He had to sell his equipment and get out. Grandma and Grandpa were livid for years. They lectured Dad and told him he should never have moved from his previous location. I don't remember the specifics, but their initial outrage must have been dramatic. My memory is hazy and I am sure we grandchildren weren't present when Dad broke the news to them, but during later visits the failure was a hot topic of debate. I was present during one of Grandma's tantrums, and later we collectively informed Mom of her remarks. Only then did Mom explain with greater clarity that the main reason Grandma and Grandpa were mad was because they had given Dad the down payment for the Elbur home, and after he sold it and moved us to a less expensive house, he took the profit from the sale to help start up the new store. Everything was gone.

I think that as time went on they realized how harsh they had been toward Dad, because on subsequent visits they would remark, "[So and so] stopped by today and they miss your meat." I recall another conversation in which Dad found out about a truck driver who had driven in from a long way just to get Dad's kielbasa and was very disappointed he could not get it anymore. It was really hard on Dad to lose his livelihood. He was never the same; in fact, he started getting worse.

Dad decided to try to find a job in sales with the new meat distributors and he did. He worked for two of them before giving up on everything. The first was Superior Meats. When he was fired from that job, he took another with Wilson Meats (or vice versa, I don't recall which company was first). He came home and complained about his bosses and how the territories were not fair and that they favored certain sales reps. He complained about not being trained well enough to be a success. When he came home in his white short-sleeved shirt and black dress pants each day, I was periodically given the duty of taking his shirt down to wash in the washtub. The only thing that would get his sweat stains out of his collar and from under his arm pits was a good dose of bleach. But I figured out that too much bleach would ruin the fabric so I started mixing Tide with a little bleach and added another secret ingredient—elbow grease. The stains would safely come out every time. My little trick earned me the privilege of making Dad's shirt-cleaning a part of my regular household duties. This added duty lasted two stints of several months each. I had a short reprieve between his jobs, and I remember wishing he would lose the second job so I wouldn't have to clean his shirts. I felt terrible when he was fired from the second sooner than the first. Before, Dad had always had his shirts dry-cleaned. They came back folded in a nice box with the perfect amount of starch. Dad was particular about the starch. Everything was changing but not for the better.

After Dad lost his second job, he seemed to fall apart. He would go across the street and not come home until well after we had gone to bed. At first we kids didn't know he had developed a bad drinking problem, but it became more and more apparent. He would start verbally attacking everyone no matter what they were doing or saying. He would hit a lot but more with the back of his hand across the cheek or a kick in the butt as you walked away if he felt like it. He had stopped strapping us, though, and I know about when that happened, but I am not exactly sure why.

Kids love bright colors. Mom was a smoker. She would buy boxes of matches and we were always curious what the covers would look like when she opened them. One day she came home from the store with matches that had bright, florescent colors. "Wow," I thought, "those are so cool." But I never lit one in any place other than the kitchen. However, Isabelle, my younger sister born in 1964, who was about five or six at the time, didn't understand that they were dangerous. We didn't know they were missing because Mom brought home so many of them. Time passed and the cool matches were almost gone. One day Mom asked me to put some clothes away after the laundry was done. I opened a drawer in Isabelle's dresser and there they were! Oh my gosh, I couldn't believe it. My first reaction was the one I should have gone with: take them out and show them to Mom and tell her where I found them.

But unfortunately another idea sprung to mind. I decided not to get Isabelle in trouble and figure out another way. (Mom sometimes would dole out harsh punishments and who knew what Dad would do.) So I got Genevieve and Isabelle and I told Isabelle she was going to get in trouble if she didn't put them back. Isabelle begged us not to tell Mom, but she did not want to put them back. I asked her why she had them and she said, "I like the colors." I suggested that we light them that night after going to bed. That way no evidence would remain. We all seemed okay with this plan. Well, like clockwork, Isabelle was sent to bed and I followed shortly thereafter. Genevieve seemed content to stay downstairs so I left her. After a respectable amount of time had passed, I ventured into Isabelle's room and said, "Isabelle, wake up. We need to light the matches." I think I had a little pyromania or something going on in my head, but this seemed like the only way to solve the problem. We started lighting them and soon we were oohing and aahing over the spectacle. We would light one book and then add another as that one fizzled out. We were almost done when, a split second after a lit match had just fizzled out, Isabelle leaned in and the hot tip of it touched her skin. I quickly moved it away, but she screamed out, and that was that!

Mom flew up the stairs and into the room, with my brother and sisters right behind. The lights went on and I was pulled out of the room into the front bedroom and the door was closed behind and someone said, "Wait 'till Dad gets here." I was petrified.

The door to the room was ajar and I tried to observe and listen to what was going on with Isabelle. Why was she crying so much when the match barely touched her? Mom demanded butter, which quickly materialized, and she liberally applied it to the burn. Dad came up and his first question was, "Bonnie, what happened?" Then, "How is her eye?" I was alarmed and concerned. The match hadn't got anywhere near her eye. I knew then that Isabelle had overreacted to the burn, but as an adult I now realize her reaction was normal. She was probably really scared.

Dad came into the room. As soon as he did, I started screaming. I turned around to take the strapping position and placed my hands, palm sides out over my butt, as though I could protect myself. I screamed and jumped up and down. At first Dad started looking for his thick strap but couldn't find it. Then I noticed he was going for the strap around his waist, but he wasn't wearing one. Then he sat on the bed and watched me scream and slowly I began to realize he wasn't going to hit me. He didn't say a word. He just put his face in his hands. I guess he thought that I had already got my licking so further punishment wasn't necessary. I don't know what was going through his mind, but he did not move and he did not hit me. As the realization came to me that he wasn't going to strap me, I suddenly felt safe and then concerned for him. I approached him and said, "Dad, are you okay?" He said, "Go." He never used a strap excessively again on any of us.

Isabelle had a little skin scar next to her eye for a long, long time. It eventually disappeared, and she had no damage to her cornea or any part of her eye. The relief I felt over the years grew; but every time I looked at her then and noticed first the scabbed wound and later the pallid demarcation of the scarred remains, I felt remorse for my actions. The incident left other scars. Many years later I came to realize that Isabelle thought I was a bad person, and she never really seemed to trust me. She wouldn't agree with anything I said or did. It was all wrong, and throughout our youth it would never change. As an adult she eventually forgave me (I believe but don't know for sure), and I think she loves me. She calls and sings "Happy Birthday" to me over the phone every year. She also calls to talk once every couple of years. Time heals all wounds it is said, but God grants miracles too, and I thank Him for intervening somehow. I would like to believe Isabelle forgave me after all.

Denison—Family Life

I have not divulged other aspects of being from a big family. First, we were somewhat of an oddity, like a "cheaper by the dozen" phenomenon. When we were all at church, we would take up almost a whole row. Heads always turned as we entered our pew. We noticed others the same way back—it was typical—but we were known for being a large family. Dad used to take us shoe shopping together so he could get a deal. He would take us in and of course we needed shoes. We only had our tennis shoes and school shoes. He would take us either to Joe's on Lorain Avenue or Sabo's Shoes across from the mall—wherever he could get the best deal. The clincher was we couldn't get the trendy shoes. The manager would always give Dad a price break for the shoes fewer people purchased. I am sure he realized Dad was tight on money having so many kids, and as a matter of fact, Dad used this as a negotiating strategy. It was embarrassing, but somehow I realized the managers seemed somewhat amused by and obviously sympathetic toward Dad. They cut him deals. So the girls all walked out with brown and white saddle shoes, except Bonniemarie. She not only didn't want them, she was visibly upset that she would have to wear them when all the other girls wore black and white ones. I think Dad had to let her pick out something else anyway because her feet were so big—size eleven—and she got penny loafers. Sabo's was the only shoe store that carried shoes in her size.

Mom figured into our growing up years in so many ways. One was her sudden interest in starting us on our own collections. I was on the sidelines when Mom broached the subject one day, saying, "Bonniemarie, I think you should collect dolls." Bonniemarie smiled in delight. "Would you like to collect cup and saucer sets?" she asked Faith. "China ones would be the best." She looked around but Faith wasn't there. "Where's Faith?" Two of us shuffled away and ran upstairs to find her. We told Faith Mom's idea on our way downstairs to join the others. Mom repeated her collection idea to Faith and asked what she thought. Faith nodded her head in the affirmative and seemed quite pleased with Mom's choice. I wanted to be included so I asked Mom what I could collect. I don't think she was prepared for this. Since I was young, someone piped in, "How about stuffed animals?" Mom said, "That may work." I was somewhat disappointed because I had never been a toy-loving kid. But that was my first collection.

As time went on, Mom saw that I had outgrown stuffed animals, and the hobby proved impractical because of the space they took up. So when I was about eleven, figurines became my new collection. I was relieved to be finished with the stuffed animals but did not quite understand what a figurine was, so I asked. Grandma Braun was there at the time and was the first to respond to my query. "Amzy, a figurine is a glass figure," she said. That was the only description I got. "I have some in the cabinet at my house. You've seen them." I really had never noticed them before, but Grandma's tone implied that I should remember them, so I just said, "Oh, okay," pretending to understand. Well, within a day or two, I did know what they were because Mom gave me two. I put them in my room and stared at them. One, a girl in a huge yellow bonnet, was no bigger than three inches high, and truthfully, I don't remember what the other one was but it was also yellow. Yellow became my favorite color for a long time after that. My collection grew over the years. Each figurine was unique in terms of its appearance. Some were collections within a collection. For example, one Christmas Mom gave me Disney's version of the seven dwarves. For the subsequent Christmas, I received Donald Duck, his wife, Daisy, and Huey, Dewey, and Louie. I think I got Peter Pan that year too.

I still felt unsettled about collecting. I was around when Mom discovered a good find for Bonniemarie—she picked up a Shirley Temple doll. Bonniemarie was delighted with it when she opened it that Christmas. It went upstairs to join the special group she kept there. Then one day Mom came home with news. She had been out with friends and told them about the collections. Bonniemarie's Shirley Temple doll acquisition came up. One friend informed Mom that if the manufacturer's insignia was on the doll's bottom, it was an authentic, first-edition doll and was very valuable. This was the first time I understood that Mom had us collecting for a reason other than providing each of us with a different collection. I envied Bonniemarie then and thought she had the best collection. But I never let on that I did not really care for collecting. I went along, always accepting my gifts and showing appreciation.

Today I look back and think, Mom really gave us each a unique gift. Through collecting I learned the value of detail, especially in art and ceramics. I learned that even though each thing can have its own intrinsic value because it is unique, that value can increase because of an item's age or popularity or the quality of the workmanship. I learned that some collectibles cost more than others but aren't necessarily worth more over time. I learned that the age of something kept in pristine condition can factor into value. I (and, I would like to believe, my sisters as well) learned valuable lessons because of our collections. I wonder if Mom had all of this in mind. Probably she fathomed some of it, but I think what Mom wanted most was for us to always wonder about the value of something and realize that value can come from what we think about it and how we care for it and not from how others necessarily determine its worth.

There was a holiday that made having so many siblings a bonus: Christmas with a tree surrounded by gifts of all sizes wrapped in an unending assortment of wrapping paper—red and gold with a blue ribbon or red and green with a white ribbon, it didn't matter—we all loved it and wondered which presents were from Santa and which were from others. Even though we each only got small items, they added up. We all looked like good kids to Santa—that was for sure. We would start opening gifts around six p.m. and it would take until midnight to open them all. If we weren't too tired, we would all get ready and head off to midnight mass. Each gift was opened by the recipient under the scrutiny of everyone else. Usually we had Mom's parents with us, but sometimes both sets of grandparents were on hand. So gift-giving took that much longer. If you counted seven items on average per kid and added a few for each of the parents and grandparents, then at least sixty to seventy gifts were piled around the tree each year.

Mom used to disappear a night here or a night there, and we always wondered where she was going. We would try to guess. Faith suggested she was Christmas shopping. Bonniemarie figured Mom was going to Grandma's to wrap gifts, but that didn't stop them from searching the house to see if Mom was wrapping gifts at home. She did that too. Mom was a great gift-giver. We would always get a lot of stuff we needed, but somehow she would include that one special thing we wanted forever. My family unwittingly gave me one unique package from each of these annual gift-giving fests: happy memories full of wonder, love and laughter.

We shared another large family experience that we knew then and still agree now was really comical. For years Dad went nuts over Volkswagens. He thought it was a very good car so he bought a punch buggy (a nickname for the Beetle). All nine of us would pile into the car to go places. Every time we got in or out, friends and family would look on and laugh. They couldn't believe we all fit in. We thought it was funny too and never seemed embarrassed by it. I think Dad owned several in succession. They varied in color—white, blue, and black. Regardless of color, size matters.

We also stood out—which obviously wasn't hard to do—when Mom made the girls matching outfits for Easter Sunday. One year we all wore dresses with matching capes Mom made using her sewing machine. She would search the pattern section of the local fabric store and find the perfect outfits to sew. This time she found us each a pattern that included a cape, a dress, a blouse, and a skirt. Each cape was a different color: I wore blue; Bonniemarie had yellow; Faith, green; and Genevieve, red. We each had a dress one year and a skirt/blouse set the next. The capes matched both outfits. The blouse was the same print as the inside of the cape. The skirt was the solid match for the outside of the cape. Mom did something cool. She made it so the capes were reversible. What a spectacle we must have been. Another year she couldn't manage to sew, but she was able to buy us matching dresses. They all were short-sleeved and primarily navy blue with a white and green stripe going down the front. We looked good wearing these and got many compliments. I know we turned quite a few heads each year, bringing smiles and looks of amazement from onlookers.

Denison—Fights & Fears

Thoughts creep into my mind about some of the events I need to include from my life, about how they may impact my family, and I know I will need to camouflage them in the end...

Family life had the appearance of normalcy, but my parents were struggling financially, and gradually all the extras at Christmas dwindled away to necessities with one of us getting a "surprise" gift, which usually was something we really wanted (not needed) from Santa; but sometimes this special gift fulfilled both criteria—like the Christmas Bonniemarie got a large suitcase because she would soon leave for college.

In order to supplement the family income, my parents decided to convert our basement area into a rental apartment. We were all told to go downstairs and clean out the two rooms which would constitute the main living area. We had an old kitchen table and a couch downstairs, which my parents thought they should leave so they could call it a furnished apartment. This pronouncement made them realize it may be better to furnish the entire area as best they could. I believe our grandparents donated a bed, an old metal wardrobe, and a mirrored dresser to complete a furnished bedroom. The outside wall of this room abutted our patio off the back of the house.

The laundry room, with its broken washing machine and dryer, doubled as a kitchen of sorts. [Due to the fact that the washing machine and dryer were broken, we were already doing our laundry across the street, so the only time we would encroach upon this space would be when we needed to hang wet clothing on the line. Thank goodness the Laundromat was so close]. There was no stove, but there were cupboards and a mini-counter under it with drawers, and an old fridge.

The furnace room had a huge, old coal furnace which had never been removed and had somehow been converted, which I never completely understood. In the corner adjacent to the furnace stood a small wall sink and a potty, which sat inside a wooden picket-like enclosure the size of a bathroom stall for the handicapped. A metal shower was off in another corner of the furnace room. This was a great spot for a bathroom because it was by far the warmest section of the house throughout the winter months.

The future tenant would have everything he or she needed. My parents advertised, but before doing so they deliberated over the amount they would ask for rent. I don't recall what the asking price was, but I do know they had to lower the price to get and keep renters. We kids were a noisy and nosey bunch so the lack of privacy was an issue; the fact that it was a basement apartment was another; and really, even though we thought the space looked great, you had to be desperate to live there. I know some renters came and went, but the last and final one stayed the longest. She was a nice lady with blonde hair she over-teased and sprayed. She was short and in her late fifties or early to mid-sixties. I don't remember her name—let's call her Helen—but she could only afford fifteen dollars per month in rent. Dad wanted to help her even though it wasn't enough money to do us much good, so she was in. She didn't complain much about the noise. The only thing she asked for was a door for the rectangular-shaped opening to her apartment. We couldn't afford to have a carpenter in to do this type of work, so Dad and Helen agreed on a better curtain for greater privacy. Mom made it and Helen seemed satisfied.

I remember romping down the staircase once in a while to hang some damp laundry, but then our parents asked us to walk quietly down the stairs. I had to get accustomed to seeing the closed curtain, which shifted slightly from the air movement caused by brisk entries down the stairs. I could always tell when Helen was there and about. I would hear a little sigh of disappointment when she heard me coming down, but she would be quiet. You could hear the TV going. I imagined her watching TV. I wanted to knock and say hello, but I didn't, knowing she wanted her privacy.

Eventually we discovered she was a barmaid from the Double A. Dad and Mom had also befriended a couple that owned a florist shop down the street, and I believe they were the people that had recommended our basement apartment to Helen. Anyway, she lived with us the longest despite the fact that one night we heard her screaming. I don't recall what time it was, but I do remember Dad heading down into the basement and a few of us kids standing in the kitchen area wondering what had occurred. As Dad was coming up, I heard Helen shout, "Get it out! It's a rat! There are rats!" Then it was quiet. Dad came up. Of course we all heard what she said. I think Dad and Sammy rounded them up somehow and took care of them. Dad needed to find a way to seal up a hole in the basement wall in the bedroom area. I don't know when he did it, but it took awhile. But I know the very next day several remedies were underway. One of them was moving our trash receptacles away from the house to an area more remote near the other side of a garage. At some point I began having dreams with human-size rats. I was afraid.

We had had a mouse get into the main living area of our house on occasion and our then dog Ginger, a collie-German shepherd mix, would start barking and soon she would be running all about trying to catch it. I hated it when this happened. I couldn't understand why we had mice. Now I realize the house could have had every rodent known to man because of its poor construction. Sometime after the mice and rat incidents, we had a particularly rainy summer and the drains and sewers were full. Genevieve and I had eventually moved into the front bedroom in the uppermost level of the house. When it poured we could hear mice crawling up the interior walls, and they would make a pounding noise on the flooring in the dual storage closets constructed on either side of the bedroom. We asked Mom to investigate. She came up, had us remove everything from the closets, saw nothing wrong with the flooring, determined it was our imaginations, and dismissed our complaints with zero action. She told us to put everything away, and she disappeared.

As the summer progressed, something else crawled into our lives; every time we went downstairs to hang clothes, we killed some kind of beetle with a really hard shell. Mom had an exterminator in. He said the mice were baby rats and we needed to do something fast to take care of them." "But," he said, "the beetles are coming up from the sewer because of how high the water levels are. They are just a nuisance and after the water goes back down, this problem will go away." In the meantime they crawled everywhere, and each time I went down in the basement, I had to get my nerve up. Then I would crush them with a wooden board before I would step in an area I needed to go in. It was gross because the shells were so hard; I could hear them crack when the board came down on them. At least they couldn't crawl on me. Before they started to disappear, they even came up through openings in the walls and got into our cereal in the lower cabinet. We had to start keeping the cereals on the kitchen counter so we didn't have to throw them away.

With the geographical adjustments Dad made for the garbage cans, we all hoped the rat invasion had resolved itself. My guess is Dad went downstairs to make sure the rats were gone. I don't recall how or when Dad repaired the wall, but I really don't think it mattered. The man that built our house had also built the house next door. He had passed away several years before we arrived on the scene, but his wife and wife's sister, I believe, lived in the second house and had sold the one we were in to the prior owner. They seemed to know all about our house, which was helpful in some ways and not in others. My father went over to ask them questions when big problems came up. This was one of them. He discovered that the inner wall of the house was not brick down into the basement area. Apparently the man had installed a concrete floor, but only beams of some nature from the basement up through the upper levels of the house. In other words, behind the dry wall was dirt. Well, the garbage had attracted the rats and they gnawed down in through a crack and then easily through the drywall. Helen must have been scared out of her wits. Dad got Helen to return by assuring her he had solved the problem. I couldn't understand that. I don't think she slept in the bedroom anymore though. I used to notice her dozing on the sofa in front of the TV.

Things steadily declined. It seemed like my parents were arguing all the time about something. All of us kids were on edge. When Dad came home we would all disappear. One of us started playing lookout. As soon as the lookout saw him coming from across the street, the lookout would warn the others and we would all run and hide. I recall Dad coming in one day and noticing. He said, "Where is everyone?" "Hi, Sam," said Mom. "Hi," Dad said, "Where is everyone, Bonnie?" "I don't know," Mom replied. She knew we all had disappeared to hide from him.

I had only made my way into the living room, so I decided to try to sneak around through the kitchen and go upstairs. Mom came into the kitchen following Dad. He started doing something at the sink to take care of his fish tanks. I quickly backpedaled through the living room and started toward the stairs to the upper level. I heard Mom start an argument with Dad. She was telling him that we kids were afraid of him and we hid when we knew he was coming. He didn't like it, and then she started telling him that he wasn't making any money and…SLAP. I heard the noise and then Mom cried out, "Stop, don't hit me, Sam!" I quickly came back down the stairs, stopping at the bottom and looking into the kitchen, I saw that Dad had a hold on Mom and looked like he was about to punch her in the cheek. She moved to try and stop him. I came up to him to scream, "Leave her alone, Dad. Stop hitting her." You need to understand that I was very afraid of my father's unpredictable moods, and even though I was telling my mind to scream to stop him, the sound of my voice did not come out loudly; but the tone of an angry, frightened, and nervous scream was absolutely present in the sound that first caught in my throat and then emerged into the threatening air. I wanted him to stop hurting her.

He seemed to release his grip, and I thought he was going to come after me. I ran down in the basement and into the arms of Helen. It was like she was waiting there for me. She had heard everything. She held me and let me cry in her arms. She said, "Don't worry. It'll be okay now." As I got a hold of myself, I thanked her and realized I needed to go back upstairs and see how Mom was. I went up, and Helen came up shortly too. Mom was sitting on the stairs that led to the second level of the house. She had her face in her hands and she was crying. Dad left after he realized what he had done. I had Mom move her hand so I could see; her face was turning black and blue where Dad had hit her. A couple of my siblings arrived on the scene. Mom was strong. She said she was okay; she would be black and blue. A call was made to Grandma Braun. They talked. I don't remember everything very clearly after this. I think Mom went to Grandma's, and perhaps we all did.

Within a couple weeks of this incident, a family meeting convened. We were all asked to sit around the dining room table. I think it was us kids that called the meeting. We all came out with it. We all said we were afraid of Dad. Mom asked if we wanted him to move out and we all said "Yes." It was unanimous. "Well," Mom said, "I guess I need to tell him." (I know there was more discussion revolving around Dad's removal from the house, but I don't recall who said what or how each of my siblings felt and why. I do remember that we were all concerned enough for Mom's safety that we did not want to give Dad a second chance and hurt Mom even worse. Sometimes life with Mom wasn't that great either, but she didn't deserve to be hit.)

I recall Mom telling Dad a week or two or perhaps a month later (the timing of the event is not clear) and adding her own punch to the "You have to get out, Sam" message. She filed for a separation, which included a court order that he had to move out within so many days. He could take all of his clothes and any of his belongings he wished with him. He had to hand over his key to the house, which I think he did right at that moment. Then I think he pleaded with her to change her mind, but she was adamant. She said she had given him plenty of chances, and he always said he was going to change, but he didn't. This time he would not be forgiven. He had to get out.

Here is an interesting tidbit. Mom visited recently. Since I was writing this story and considering possible modes of presentation, I decided that I would try to fill in some gaps of memory to clarify things that I may not have totally understood as a child or young adult. I asked, "Mom, do you remember the day Dad hit you?" She said, "Yes." I prompted, "Can you tell me what your recollections were of this timeframe?" Without hesitation, like it was only yesterday, she said, "I was always nagging Dad about something and when he came in from across the street, he went in the kitchen to do something with the fish. I followed him in and started complaining about the fact that he needed to get a job. I pushed him over the edge."

I realized she had come to terms with the serious nature of her behavior and actions during that time. I always had a modicum of disrespect for Mom until that moment. "Your father was depressed, and he needed help." She saw that her badgering nature had contributed to the explosive way he reacted. Dad may have fared differently if only people directly involved with him, including Mom, had tried to help him. Mom went on to tell me how his parents, especially Grandma, were always ridiculing Dad, saying, "He was one of three boys. Sam could never get it right in their minds. Uncle Frank was the great one until Uncle Gordon got older, and then he became the favorite. Sam was always doing the wrong thing and they never let him think otherwise." It's ironic. Dad was the only son to give them grandchildren. He should have been the greatest for this achievement alone. This may be another reason why I never thought we mattered, especially me.

I realize today that many of those attacks on character had been inculcated into our family dynamic. We had so many fights growing up, and we were always trying to say it was the other guy's fault. Sibling rivalry is a normal dynamic with kids, and I have come to realize this as I watch my own children behaving in this fashion from time to time. But with more kids it was more frequent because any combination of incidents could trigger a fight, and depending on this combination, the intensity would vary. For example, I eluded to the fact that Genevieve and Faith seemed to be chums and leave me out. Well, this happened on numerous occasions throughout childhood, not just with Maria Savage. This was compounded by the fact that Mom tended to side with certain other siblings and leave me out of major decisions. Then when it came time to go somewhere or do something as a family, I would be the last to find out. So I would say, "I didn't know about this." The response would be, "Well, Amzy, if you were around or you listened when we talked about it, then you would know." This was totally unrealistic. I didn't hang out with them all the time because they were so boring I could just throw up. They probably knew how I felt and found their own way to give it back to me. This made my life a misery. They would never hit the subject head-on, and I was too young to know I should. It wasn't until about seven years ago and a recent move that my oldest sister intervened on my behalf and turned Mom around with regard to her unjust treatment of me relative to this bad habit of excluding me, then making me look like an ogre. Bonniemarie saw how wrong it was of Mom to do this to me, and she just stepped into my life and corrected it. I don't think I would be on good terms with Mom today if Bonniemarie hadn't done so. I need to thank her for this and I will.

Returning to the topic of sibling rivalry, simple arguments over silly things could escalate into pushing, punching, and scratching fests. I ran from these outbursts as soon as I could, but they always began with someone either inadvertently or intentionally doing something that bothered another, followed by an attempt by one party to gain superiority by shouting, the situation perhaps escalating into physical attacks, or the two together. These fights became punishable for the party that started it. The problem for both parents was determining who was at fault. They often decided without proof that Sammy and Faith were the culprits; Bonniemarie was very good at assessing their involvement and whitewashing herself from the crime, so they very often bore the brunt of the punishments doled out for seemingly bad behavior. It confused me to see them getting punished, and I didn't know how I could defend them. Afraid that I would somehow be implicated in the event, I would slink away and become invisible for awhile. I got good at that.

Only recently in my life when the "It's your fault" option creeps into my conversation and the other party is feeling attacked have I attempted to quickly move the dialogue in a direction of an explanatory nature. "It wasn't your fault," I'll interject, "these things just happen, but what's more important is what we do about it." This usually moves the conversation in a more constructive direction; but sometimes the damage is already done. When the attack is on me, however, I have major issues. I become confused and feel like I need to mount a counterattack; but I usually let the person have their moment, become silent, and continue with what I was doing, dismissing the incident; or either I or they walk away. My feelings are not resolved then and there because I am afraid of losing that friend or making a scene or saying the wrong thing. I get truly tongue-tied—my tongue can't pronounce the thoughts in my head and the thoughts in my head are so jumbled that they cannot come out of my mouth correctly. It takes me too long to react, and the opportunity to repair the situation usually disappears or gets worse. If I can I'll try to fix things by phone because I feel less threatened, but if the other party is mad enough, this does not help. People don't realize what a good person I truly am. I hope I can someday learn to cope better with this flaw.

Dad gathered his things and left with a couple suitcases full of stuff and perhaps a couple boxes of things as well. Over the next few weeks, we all needed to adjust to the fact that Dad was gone and that we didn't have to be afraid anymore of him coming home. You could almost see relief float through the house. We could all feel it, that's for sure. It felt good.

Denison—Out in the Cold

Well, life didn't return to normal. Things changed. Mom had to make several trips to the courthouse to finalize things. The separation was going to turn into a divorce. Mom cited that she knew he was never going to change and that the financial situation was beyond their control. She hoped that with Dad gone she would become eligible for welfare and other government subsidies so she could put food on the table and get a better job. I didn't know what welfare was, but I knew Mom was okay with it, so I asked. She explained that the government gives families food stamps and financial assistance when they are in extreme need. But we would have to wait six months before we would get anything. Why didn't they understand we needed the money yesterday?

Winter set in and I remember that when it got cold, all of a sudden the heat went off. I couldn't believe it. How could this happen? So this is what my siblings and I did to survive the cold. We put as many blankets as possible on our beds. Sometimes at night we would double up two or more to a bed for body heat. We would have our winter coats handy, and in the morning we would put them on and run down to the kitchen. Faith was usually up early and she would go into the kitchen, close the two entry doors, and turn on the gas oven (somehow we still had heat from a gas oven, but I don't get how). The kitchen was warm and toasty, a welcome relief. After we warmed up and ate something, we would run upstairs and get dressed as fast as we could. Finally one day Mom came home and said welfare came through. We had heat again and food stamps.

I'll never forget feeling proud of the fact that we could afford food again. This soon changed. I gradually realized that people acted somewhat differently when they served us. I noticed it especially when we stood in line and I heard the change in the cashier's conversational tone. The cashier would get serious. She would ring everything up carefully and then announce the dollar amount of the transaction. Mom would take out her wallet and the food stamps and start counting out the money. She got to the point where she knew how much was in a book and she would hand them several books and a couple extra from another for the balance. They would count back change in food stamps too. You would never get real money for change. Mom would tell them to forget the change if it was under a dollar. It was weird, but that's how it was.

During Mom's recent visit, I brought up another event which needed clarification, thinking her perspective would enlighten me. "Mom, I need to ask you about something else. I hope you can help me." She said, "I'll try, Amzy."

"Why didn't we have any heat that one winter? You remember, Mom. I guess I don't know if I remember correctly. What I do remember is that Faith would go down to the kitchen and turn on the heat in the stove and close both doors. Then when we woke up, we would all run down into the kitchen. How could we not have heat in the house but have a gas stove that worked? I must not remember right."

Mom said, "Oh yes, I remember you kids and me sleeping in sleeping bags downstairs." "But, Mom, not just that, I remember us doubling up in beds and getting up and having our winter coats next to the beds so we could put them on in the mornings when we got up. And I remember running down to the kitchen to get warm. Why was the kitchen warm and the rest of the house cold?" Mom looked at me and realized I had a point.

She said, "Amzy, I don't remember everything and you're right, it doesn't seem to make sense. When we applied for welfare and it finally came through, the welfare people explained the benefit system to me. They said we could not use the food stamps for anything other than food. The furnace broke and we had no money to fix it. Grandma and Grandpa wanted to fix it, but I didn't want them to pay for it. But they insisted, and I let them pay to fix it. It was a lot of money. That was why we had no heat then."

I couldn't believe it. Mom's pride got in the way of what made sense for our survival. I know this was a simplistic way of looking at it, but that was a very scary episode in our lives. Mom's pride got in the way of accepting help to fix a bad situation: She wouldn't ask for a handout, and when her parents offered help, she almost refused it. But she didn't.

Mom had had a lot on her plate then, and she needed some time to understand how to handle things. It must have been hard because she had to do everything on her own. She is not a left-brain person so it took her longer. Upon reflection I think it's amazing that we all made it to adulthood, married nice men (or in the case of my brother, a great woman), and lead relatively normal lives.

I was twelve when Mom and Dad's divorce became final. Mom came home and explained and she seemed happy. Again, I think we were all relieved that we were one step more removed from Dad. But then the clincher: Dad had visitation rights, although the older kids didn't have to see Dad unless they chose to; Mom thought Sammy should see Dad every once in awhile. But Dad had visitation rights with the children under thirteen. That meant me and my younger siblings had to go with him once a week. For me at least it was for only a year. I was scared. It was decided we would see him on Sundays. I only had to see him for an hour, but my siblings had to visit for at least three, so some of my visits were extended. I recall that as time progressed Dad occasionally brought me back after an hour and continued his visit with my other siblings.

The first visit with Dad after the divorce was approaching. He called and arranged a one p.m. pickup with Mom. We would be coming with him to Grandma's. He wanted us to dress nicely, so we did.

I was afraid. I remember my sisters leaving the house and going to his car. I was the last one to go. I didn't want to, but Mom said I had to, so I finally went out. It was quiet. Dad made some small talk with my sisters. He seemed so happy to see Tristen. Tristen, only three years old, was the youngest and cutest. She had been a surprise baby.

One other memory I neglected to share earlier was the fact that Tristen was more than a surprise. Mom was done having kids, but one night when Dad had had too much to drink, he went to bed shortly after Mom. I happened to come upstairs (I think by then Genevieve and I had been moved up to the third floor.

It really did end up being a place for "the girls." Sammy was moved down into the room at the top of the stairs that Genevieve and I had shared during our first years in this house.) Anyway, I was going up to the third level, and as I came to the hallway on the second level, I heard Dad through the walls harassing Mom, saying, "C'mon Bonnie, I have needs too." Mom groaned and was pushing Dad away, saying, "Get off, Sam. No, Sam. No." Then it sounded like a little fight where Mom was really trying to get Dad off of her and she was not happy. Then it was quiet. I went upstairs. Many years later I realized that Dad had forced himself on Mom. Then there was Tristen, the youngest of seven. It was 1968.

Denison—Adolescence

The divorce happened in 1971—as I said, when I was twelve—and I was just trying to grow up and have a normal life. It seemed to me at the time that the popular girls at school were thin, wore makeup, and traveled in groups. I was not allowed to wear makeup, I was not thin (everyone remarked that I had a medium bone structure), and I did not hang with a group. I decided to change things. I started making friends with a girl at school by the name of Lorain. She was friendly and confident. She also at times would talk with a group of girls. One girl's name was Kristy, and I started making friends with her too. We seemed to get along most of the time. Kristy invited me over to her house once and I met her mother. Her mom mostly spoke directly to Kristy, but once or twice tried to include me in the conversation. Then Kristy asked if we could visit in her room and her mom said yes. So off we went. We didn't visit long, but I remember Kristy started talking about how she was already developing (which was apparent). I felt five years old all of a sudden because I had no breasts. She continued, telling me about the fact that she was getting pubic hair and how much she had. I thought this was a little gross, but she was very matter-of-fact about it so I didn't overreact. It seemed like we didn't have too much in common. I don't think the visit lasted too much longer. Her mom wanted to leave to run an errand.

Anyway, getting back to changing things, gradually I had this group of friends: Lorain, Kristy, Ann, Cindy, and me. A girl named Tammy and some others mingled with us at times, but we five were a steady group.

Next, I saw that I needed to lose weight. I would look at magazines, especially at Tammy's house; the models were all so thin. I started cutting out snacks after school, and if we missed a meal at home, I just didn't eat anything to make up for it. If we had popcorn at night, I skipped it. I stopped drinking pop because it had sugar, and milk because it had fat in it. When dinner time came, I ate very small portions of food. Lent came and I gave up meat and sugary treats. Slowly the pounds started coming off. When I weighed in at 105 pounds, down from 120, I felt I was good. But I stopped getting my period and Mom took me to the doctor. He examined me and said I was fine and told Mom that it was common for young girls to have irregular periods. He said it would probably start up again in a year. I was happy there was nothing wrong and I felt validated.

Mom spoke to me privately on a few occasions after this, urging me to eat more. She said I was getting too thin and she was worried about me. At first, I thought, "Oh, she just wants me to get fat because she is jealous." Then I saw the concern of my sisters, especially Genevieve. She said I was too skinny and I looked bad. I thought she was probably jealous too. Over time, though, I realized that if this was the opinion of several people, perhaps I had taken my diet a bit too far. I started eating a little more. Some of my energy levels returned and I didn't need so many naps. This was good. I stayed thin for the next several years, but my periods did come back a year later just like the doctor predicted. So I had a group of friends and I was thin.

I don't think I was ever as popular as the other girls, but I started to see that boys were talking to me and noticing me, so it didn't matter. Once the boys started to get to know me better, a few of them commented about some of the popular girls. They would say very unpleasant things and alluded to that fact that one of these girls was doing "fooling around" things with boys, and the boys really didn't respect her at all. They would go hang at her house just to get some. Then I would hear what they liked. They all liked one girl named Candy Runyon, and they wanted her to notice and like them. She had a twin brother whom I liked, but he never noticed me (as far as I know). But hearing what the boys liked, I knew they probably liked me too. I was quiet and nice like Candy but not a boy chaser or easy like other girls, two traits they didn't like. Once or twice a couple boys went home my way and tried to talk to me on the way. Looking back now I realize that that was as good as it got. But back then I didn't know this and I was still insecure about whether or not boys liked me. I didn't know how I could be popular because I wasn't a cheerleader and most of the boys ignored me—especially the ones I thought were cute! I was a quiet girl so in reality how could they ever get to know me? It was impossible.

Once our parents were divorced, other changes occurred; for one thing Mom's sewing days were definitely over. Mom was now the new dad and mom. I have wondered as a mother of only two how Mom did it for all of us. Exhaustion is part of my vocabulary, and I am fortunate enough to have a good husband who has always been able to care for us financially. I am blessed that I was able to stop working and raise our children when my oldest was seven. Mom had none of that. She had a great mom and dad herself, though, and they pitched in to help out whenever Mom needed it—and even when she didn't. Mom was lucky. Grandma would come and watch us and we started going to Grandma and Grandpa's for frequent visits and for meals. When I turned eighteen, Mom couldn't handle living on her own anymore and we moved in with Grandma. Grandpa had passed away from lung cancer about four years earlier, so Grandma was living alone. Grandma welcomed Mom and the rest of us that remained—Bonniemarie was off to college, Sammy was a whole story that I will soon disclose, and Faith had just married; so it was Genevieve, myself, Isabelle and Tristen. I was to leave for college that coming August. Thank goodness I did not have to live in the small house under two sets of rules (Mom's and Grandma Braun's) for too long.

Denison—High School

Let's back up a little. We lived in the Denison house for several years before Mom finally sold it; then we spent two or three years living in a duplex in a nicer section of the Cleveland area bordering Lakewood.

Mom had to work and eventually she found secretarial jobs. She had apparently worked as a secretary for a short time before she married Dad, having taken several classes in high school to prepare for this. She got hold of a manual typewriter and started practicing to get her typing speed back up. Then she put together a resume and started looking at the want ads. Eventually she found a job but her income was not great. The hard part was that she needed to report it to the welfare folks, who informed her that her welfare benefits would be reduced as a result of her income. She would still just barely be making ends meet.

We girls were given duties in the house. Since Bonniemarie was already on her own finishing up college, she was out of the picture. I recall that one of my jobs off and on was to come home and prepare dinner. I was excited and frightened by the responsibility of this. Over the years I had watched Mom prepare some basic meals, so this is where I started. Macaroni with ground meat and stewed tomatoes was one of our favorites and easy to make. Another one that worked was meat loaf. Spaghetti was also quick and simple. It wasn't too hard because Mom would go over the options and usually the necessary ingredients were on hand. I don't recall having to run to the store, but I am sure I did from time to time. With the Open Pantry a few doors down, it was always easy to get whatever else we needed to make a meal.

The hardest part of Mom coming home after six p.m. was when we had fights. We would call Mom and she would need to intervene so we could settle a dispute. At some point this situation got out of hand because I remember Mom telling us we had to stop calling her at work; the boss did not like all the personal calls. We didn't feel we called her that much but tried harder to settle our disputes without Mom's help. I think we did okay. If I don't remember otherwise, then we must have. Mom's first job lasted almost two years, but she needed to make more money so she started looking for a new job.

She soon found another secretarial job, but I don't recall where or how long it lasted. Then she applied to Erieview Catholic High School, got a job, and worked as the office secretary there for six or seven years. My older sisters had attended St. Augustine Academy in Lakewood, taking public transportation to get there. We all got used to public transportation. It was very reliable and affordable, if you lived in the city. I decided not to follow in my older sisters' footsteps and attend their school. They didn't seem happy there with the other girls and their friendships. Also, our cousins went there and this created some competition between them. Cousin Natalie was close to my age and I certainly didn't want to deal with the same anxieties my sisters had suffered. Besides, the Augustine girls seemed distant and unfriendly during open house. In addition my cousins had an easier life than we did, though sometimes I didn't understand why. What was clear was that their dad had a better job than our dad ever had; the cousins all wore nice clothes, and my uncle could obviously afford to send them to private school.

After visiting St. Augustine, I decided to look at other high schools. I thought about Erieview because Mom worked there and I figured it might be nice. A recruiter had come to our class and I had liked the presentation. I went to an open house and really liked the atmosphere and the girls, who were open, friendly, and truly interested in making high school a good experience. I also liked that I would be going to school in the city. It seemed exciting.

I wondered how we would pay my tuition. I told Mom I would get a job to help pay for high school. She was delighted.

The summer of my eighth grade year I applied for and obtained a part-time job through a jobs program for kids. I don't remember the specifics, but you were eligible if your parents didn't make too much money, I think. I ended up working at Erieview, which was kind of cool. I got to know the custodial staff really well. I cleaned every locker and every skylight in the school that summer. I lost a lot of weight doing it too. I liked being skinny. For some reason I thought I would have more friends that way. I made friends, but they could have cared less how skinny I was.

Mom had decided quite some time earlier to sell our house, so the summer after my sophomore year of high school she got everything ready. She painted the exterior of the house. I'll never forget her getting up high on the ladder to paint near the top of the house. I was afraid she was going to fall off, but she never did. We had to clean all the walls with Spic and Span. The house was really dirty and I realize now that it was probably due mostly to the fact that Mom was a smoker.

I got a part-time job working in a bakery. The boss seemed to like me and took a real interest in his employees. We went out as a group for dinners to nice restaurants. I never knew what motivated him to do this and thought he was just being nice. I discovered that my boss's wife was a collector, and I told her how Mom was trying to sell some furniture because we were moving out of our house. She asked if Mom had any mirrors and I said yes. That was it. She decided to come and see what Mom had. She asked if she could come over the following week, and a time was arranged. I think Mom had me call her and do all the arranging. Mom tried to get me to open up and be less shy around adults, and this was one way of doing it. It helped. Growing up with the "kids should be seen and not heard" philosophy had really affected me. I was always very afraid of adults. It took me becoming one and then even more time experimenting with this reality to get over these fears. But I still suffer severe anxiety attacks in the presence of authority figures. Right now I am fortunate because I don't have to work in the "real world." I manage the house, meals, kids, bills, and accounts and do any volunteer work I can that includes writing.

Anyway, Franz Bacho's wife came, and not only did she purchase a few pieces of Mom's furniture, she somehow arranged for whatever didn't sell to be picked up and taken away. She was a good lady. I would love to meet and talk with her again, but Franz Bacho ended up being a cheat. (It's weird how after you get to know people, you find out stuff you wish you hadn't.) I worked with a staff of young girls, and one older lady. The older one moved on and then it was only us young ones. At age thirteen or fourteen, I was the youngest by far. And the work permit I had obtained for the summer jobs program was still valid. I was in. I needed to wear a white dress—pretty standard in bakeries in those days—and appropriate shoes. Anyway, it really was a cool job. I ended up making good friends with one of the girls. She had me as a bridesmaid at her wedding. She married right out of high school. The oldest of the girls was in her twenties and she was a little streetwise. She only worked weekends and when she was there all the guys—old and young—were quite excited. She really had a way of getting the testosterone going. At some point one of the delivery guys started coming in and he happened to be one of the bakers' sons. I thought he was cute, but I was too shy to flirt. I would just try to catch his eye. He was oblivious. She, on the other hand, had him salivating all over her. I think he asked her out once or twice, but she reported that he was a jerk.

The bad part about this time period was that all the guys in the bakery started acting horny. One girl, who lived upstairs, was hired after the older one left. Franz Bacho called her Gypsy, which wasn't nice, but he liked talking to her a lot. I will also call her Gypsy, only because she did seem provocatively secretive and her family often moved (traits stereotypically associated with this nomadic group of people). One time Gypsy and I went to the local Woolworth that had just opened down the street. She wanted to buy panties, and somehow she convinced me to buy them too. Then, it was weird. We went back to the bakery after lunch. We didn't have too many patrons in the afternoons so we got all the counters cleaned and shined. All of a sudden Gypsy wanted to try on her underwear. She wanted me to see what I thought about how they fit. Okay, that was weird, but I came from a family of five sisters and we did weird stuff like that all the time. So we went into Franz Bacho's office—he wasn't around. . on one pair of mine and they fit fine. She tried on every pair of hers and rea don't recall even looking. I think I tried to do the exact opposite. She was checking herself out in Franz Bacho's little wall mirror for which she needed to climb up on his desk. Well, we finished and came out. Franz Bacho was still nowhere to be seen. So off we went back out front to the store. Business was really slow that day and I think we closed the store early.

A few weeks later, we discovered a hole in his office wall, and then Gypsy and I wondered if he had been peeking. I told her sometimes Franz Bacho would stand in his office, and I figured out he was watching us in the store through the reflection in the glass because he would come out and seem to know what we were doing and whether or not we had cleaned something the way he would want. It was okay, though, because we understood the importance of keeping the bakery operation clean. We were probably the best cleaning staff in town.

Anyway, unfortunately, a horny baker got to me. One day one of them, Sam, came up behind me and rubbed his body against mine. It was no accident. That was it; I was out of there.

My sister Genevieve had a job in a bakery, fast-food place located in the lower level of the terminal concourse. She was happy she was making a quarter an hour more than I. Even though I knew a quarter an hour wasn't that much more, I decided I needed a job making more money. I asked her if she thought her boss needed anyone new. She talked to him and the next thing I knew I was in at The Muffin Basket and out of Margaretta's Bakery. I was relieved. A couple years later when I ran into my good friend, she told me that Franz Bacho got Gypsy pregnant and she had to leave. Franz Bacho ended up sending her and her family away to keep the secret. I felt so bad for his wife because I really had liked the way she helped Mom.

I gradually became aware that Grandma Braun had corralled Mom's two brothers, Jake and Jonathon, into discussions about our financial situation. If I had been older, I would have found it embarrassing, but at the age I was, I was always optimistic that these discussions would benefit us. Apparently one brother, who lived out of state, was generous with his money; the other opened his home up to us and became almost a second dad. This is when I first became aware that certain professions paid more than others and learned the fine distinction between white-collar and blue-collar jobs.

One uncle was a stock broker and the other was an electrician. In today's world electricians aren't always considered blue-collar. Back then, the term "blue-collar" clearly referred to manual laborers—usually with union affiliations—in professions servicing industry. Uncle Jonathon, an electrician by trade, worked for "Ma Bell" in a supervisory capacity and may have fit in this category, but it is too long ago for me to know for sure. Grandma told me that electricians made good money. All I really knew was that my cousins were doing fine and, of course, we weren't. Owing to Grandma's prompting, Uncle Jonathon spoke to my aunt about helping us, which both uncles did.

Uncle Jake paid our tuitions, but it wasn't until I was a junior that Genevieve overheard a discussion between Mom and Grandma about the mysterious donor. Mom told Grandma that she had discovered that Uncle Jake had been paying my older sisters' tuitions. She had gone to the office one day to make a payment, and the office person had to leave momentarily. Mom saw a letter on the lady's desk with Uncle Jake's name on it; in the letter Uncle Jake requested that the school inform the family that the girls received scholarships, which was highly irregular at the high school level. Mom quickly deduced that he had paid Bonniemarie's and Faith's tuitions. Apparently the scholarships continued with me and Genevieve. After Genevieve relayed her newfound knowledge, she stated that she wanted to confront Mom. I was afraid to. Genevieve also decided it was time for us to stop giving Mom all the money we earned from our jobs to help pay the bills. She said she would handle it, and the next thing I knew I had spending money for the first time. Right then and there I decided to save as much as possible for college. I wanted to get out of this life any way I could.

Another twist in our lives occurred in this period. Mom befriended many of the clergy that comprised the staff at Erieview, her new secretarial home. She had a way of making people feel like family. Mom's good nature would come through after she felt comfortable with people. In many ways I inherited this trait. Mom made friends with a priest that visited the school to help counsel wayward girls. He was young, on the short side, and wore a beard and mustache. He had this little habit of thoughtfully stroking his beard and softly clicking his tongue as he engaged in conversation with people. His name was Fr. John. As the friendship grew over time, Fr. John invited Mom to see his parish. So she went. After a few visits, which Mom seemed to enjoy, he suggested that Mom bring us girls along. Mom had casually introduced me to Fr. John one day near the school office, so I knew who he was; the prospect of a visit to his church intrigued me.

Mom told us that Fr. John wanted us to meet some boys that helped out around the parish. "But," she explained, "Fr. John and I think it would be wise to prepare all of you for the fact that these boys are Blacks and come from low-income homes. Most of them do not have dads. The moms struggle to support them, but they often have drug or health problems and cannot make ends meet. This is a normal life for them, the only life they and their friends and other family members have ever known." I remember thinking, "Well, they don't seem so different from us," except I knew we had plenty of money once. I see now that that little difference in our lives—having had everything and then losing it—could possibly have made all the difference in terms of my perceptions and motivations to have a better life when I grew up.

One more point I found fascinating was that Mom didn't seem to fear these boys. She had no fear of Black people. I was surprised because I knew she had been skeptical of them at one point. Also, Dad's parents didn't speak nicely about Black people. They had once lived on the East Side on a street called Ansel Road. They moved away because the neighborhood had deteriorated and they attributed it to the fact that Black people were moving in. They couldn't sell their house because they waited too long to move and couldn't find a buyer, so they rented it. Grandpa was always complaining about the fact that they broke something he just fixed or that he had to go fix something else that broke. He said that they had no respect for property and were very destructive. Then he would also have problems collecting the rent. One time when he went by the property someone attacked him from behind, knocked him out with a blow to the head, and took his money. Grandpa was full of fear and anger toward Blacks. Some time after that, the city wanted to buy the property to make a park (which I thought was odd). They offered Grandpa only one hundred dollars for the house, but he took it, glad to let the property go. This was all I knew about Black people up until I went to high school.

Erieview, a private high school for girls, had a unique quality: it took a variety of ethnic groups. I was already acquainted with Black girls. [I would like to interject here that at this point in U.S. history, the Black community was actively attempting to break away from the stereotypes that this ethnic group determined were the fundamental reasons why Black Americans had become marginalized. One way they began changing their identity was to react strongly and with contempt to anyone who referred to them as a Negroid or nigger. They could jokingly do this among themselves, but if a Caucasian called them this, even casually, that person most likely would be branded for life as an enemy. So before going to Erieview I was tutored never to call a Black person a nigger. Of course it was not in my nature to use this term, so the lecture was unnecessary, but I was grateful for this important point of information.

Busing was a new venture in Cleveland public schools, and the reference to Blacks had to be made when debating the merits and drawbacks of this change in terms of integration in the city. Going to a private school meant Blacks and Whites chose to be together. Black Americans had been unjustly stigmatized, and various political groups were actively trying to transition them out of ghettos. One way of doing this was busing and another was to refer to them correctly in terms of their ancestral heritage. The reference to Black quickly evolved into what is now the mainstream term of African Americans.]

This ethnic group made up about a third of my class. The balance of my class was comprised of girls from a variety of ethnic backgrounds, including Slovenian, Polish, Serbian, and of course, "seventh-generation American." This is my term for any combination of ethnic backgrounds that blended into America because the families had intermarried with different ethnic groups for several generations since immigrating. Only Dad's side of the family could trace roots back to Yugoslavia and Czechoslovakia, depending on where the borders had been and when; Mom's side was a mix of German and Irish, and we don't know when her first ancestors arrived on American shores.

Anyway, we—Faith, Genevieve, Isabelle, Tristen, and I—had our visit to Trinity Parish. Fr. John was so different from any priest we had ever met. He had this little hop in his step, which we girls started to imitate and make fun of. He was totally okay with being teased about it and relished the attention by making fun of it himself in conversation. He gave a tour of the rectory first and the church later. Seeing his behind-the-scenes life brought to mind for the first time that a priest is not much different than us. He had this complex to worry about, but it didn't consume him. His philosophy seemed to be to let in anyone who wanted to be a part of running and participating in parish life. He had what business people would call an open door policy. Jesus would have approved, I remember thinking at one point. It just seemed right. I liked Fr. John.

At some point the boys' arrival seemed imminent—an adult from the area arrived at the rectory and informed someone who informed someone else who said something to Fr. John. It seemed oddly interesting to me to witness how this ripple of news made its way to Fr. John. They arrived in twos, and after four were present and we were informed that it would be awhile before the remaining boys would come, we were all quickly ushered upstairs to a large living room of sorts to meet and get to know the boys better. We were all shy at first. Fr. John made quick introductions, and then he left with Mom to do something or talk about something downstairs. I think this was for Tristen's benefit since she was only about four years old.

We got to know them. I remember Martin because we ended up liking each other. My sisters each became interested in one particular boy. It was no different than if they had been any other ethnic background. We had a nice visit. The most memorable part was that we girls all realized they were nice, they had a sense of humor, and they talked funny with each other. It was like they had their own dialect. We gently teased them about their slang, and later, discussed how they reacted. They welcomed our jests and seemed to enjoy that we noticed they were different. They promptly called us honkies. Fr. John had prepared us for this, and we knew from their tones that they did not feel offended by us at all. Over time they tried to speak more clearly around us because they wanted us to realize that they could. We could tell they had to work at it, which only served to make us respect them that much more for their unique qualities as Black people. Eventually they taught us how to do some Black dances and they in turn found ways to tease us about how we spoke.

Once they came to our house and that was quite an event. Bonniemarie had been included on an outing after this and she met two boys her age. It was like a disco when they came. They had their records, which we played. "The bump" was a type of dance done to some of their pop-style music. One of the guys said, "We are going to teach you honkies how to dance." We all laughed, and we all became quite good at moves to this dance.

After a year or so, though, the visits stopped. I think we all saw, Fr. John and Mom included, that we needed to move on. Father John was reassigned and moved to California. We exchanged letters for awhile, but they stopped. I am glad I had these interactions with a group of people that White society as a whole had shunned for reasons that were unjust. Today I enjoy people of all colors, and even though some fear of the unknown remains, I realize that each culture is unique in terms of its existence geographically, historically, and the circumstances surrounding the adventure of getting to know each of them. Fr. John was so special. He knew we weren't the most popular girls, and by carefully introducing us to these boys, we became more confident about our womanhood. These boys made us feel beautiful in every way. If I could have bottled a time in my life, this would have been it. Fr. John did good, and I really believe he knew it. I hope Martin, Simon, and all the others took something positive away from getting to know "White girls."

I need to get back to writing about my work. The Muffin Basket was a little more convenient to get to after school than Franz Bacho's bakery. I could catch a bus right outside school or, depending on my start time, walk from school to the square—about a twenty-minute walk. I usually had to start work within an hour of the end of the school day, so it was actually better to grab the bus. Often Genevieve and I met at the bus stop and rode together. The Muffin Basket had two bakery counters: one which was the other face of the fast food service counter; and the other was near the basement entrance of Higbee's. That's right, the very same Higbee's we had visited with Grandma all those years before. It's funny how life seems to take you places in ways you would never expect. I started working with the greatest person, an older lady named Fran. She was adorable. Genevieve knew I would like her and she was right. She had white hair, always wore a white uniform, and walked with a little gimp because, as she promptly explained to me, "Amzy, my right leg is slightly shorter than my left." She was quick to show me the ropes and this made me fall in love with her right away, in a manner of speaking. You just could not dislike her.

I quickly adjusted to my new job. My duties didn't involve as much cleaning as Franz Bacho's partially because we had no convenient access to water. When I started removing trays and wiping the inside of the counters, I quickly realized it wasn't as easy as it had been at Franz Bacho's. The counters were deeper and higher and the counter racks were heavier. It was much harder to complete the task because a customer could come up to the counter at any moment as they were passing to or from the concourse. As I repeatedly tried to start this chore, because we did this at Franz Bacho's, I would get sidetracked. It seemed I could never get the counters cleaned properly. Fran was ahead of me. She said, "Amzy, don't clean everything; just make sure the tops of the counters are clean. We'll wipe the fronts as we move the merchandise out at the end of the night. Don't worry. You shouldn't clean until closing. We don't want the customers to see us cleaning. They may think we're closing." She made sense. So, as I said, I quickly adjusted to the new routine.

About a month into the job, Genevieve warned me that the managing owner was going to stop over and tell me some news. I asked her, "Genevieve? What is Mr. Green's news?" Genevieve quickly responded, "They are talking about closing your bakery counter." I said, "What?" She said, "Don't worry, Amzy, Mr. Green is going to ask you if you would like to work at the main bakery near me." I was quickly relieved. The next day this is exactly what happened. He stopped over and told Fran and me that he was closing our counter because there wasn't enough business at this corner. He assured us that we would both be at the bakery adjacent to the food service counter. He asked if this was okay with us. "Of course," Fran and I said in unison. It was done.

The next evening or the next time I was scheduled to work, I went right out front instead of traveling across the concourse. I felt like I had yet another new job. I worked at The Muffin Basket throughout my high school years.

They loved Genevieve and me, especially Genevieve. We were very diligent workers. We cleaned, prepped food, and waited on folks, and I began noticing that Genevieve was very good with people. I learned a couple things from her about how to bring out the good nature of others. They always asked for her and she would get tips from certain folks on Saturdays. She coached me on what to do for so-and-so, so I could get a tip. She was so cute. She would arrange it so I could rehearse and see the results. She would say something like, "I am going to be working in the back next week prepping food, and my sister, Amzy, here is going to take care of you. Be nice to her now, would you?" Well, the person would look from her to me, at first a little anxiously, but when the patron saw the resemblance and realized Genevieve was sincere, the facial expression would soften into a smile; the person would then say okay and leave. I started getting tips too. Today the tips seem unimportant compared to this adorable memory of my sister doing this good deed. Yes, we had our fights, but I only remember the good stuff.

Working at The Muffin Basket had a depressing aspect: as we were given more responsibilities, we had to deal with the rats. One Saturday Genevieve said it was time I learned the garbage run. I was not happy about this and had hoped I would never have to do it. I think she realized how I felt. I don't recall the specifics, but the first time we went together. She said we were doing the job for Phillip (the worker who handled maintenance) because he had to leave early on some Saturdays. So we loaded all the garbage on the dolly, and she pulled and I pushed from behind toward the dump site. When I realized we were going into a remote area of the terminal complex that lacked security, I said to her, "You don't do this alone, do you, Genevieve?" She said, "No, we always go in twosomes, even Phillip." We then approached the area where a hallway led out of the complex. As we started down the darkly lit passageway, I noticed something moving along the wall. It looked huge. I said to Genevieve, "Is that a cat?" She replied, "No, let's stop. That's a rat, Amzy. We need to wait until it goes in that doorway. I think that's where it's going." I was repulsed and stunned by Genevieve's readiness to proceed. I said, "No way." She said, "Don't worry, Amzy, the rats are so big that they can't move that fast. Once it moves in that doorway, we'll just rush on past." And we did. As we went by, I looked where the rat had gone and saw that it was huge and fat. To this day I can't get over how big it was. Then we got to the garbage dump area. Ten-by-ten-feet garbage receptacles lined up near an old loading dock of sorts. The area was open to the outside, and from where we stood, you could see the river that dumped into Lake Erie.

I started to carry a huge bag of food toward one of the containers. Genevieve abruptly said in a loud voice, "Stop, Amzy. We do it like this." She took a bag and heaved it back and then launched it forward toward the top of one of the dumpsters. It landed inside and we heard scurrying noises from in or around the vats! I looked at her shocked, a little rattled, and a lot scared, and I realized she had probably saved me from getting bit by something. Then she said, "We don't get too close because of the rats." Geeze—why didn't I see that coming? I thought to myself. We quickly heaved the remainder of the bags into the vats and left. Of course we passed that one door very quickly.

Another story about The Muffin Basket involved the smaller variety of rodents—mice. Toward the end of my junior year of high school, all the local news agencies, like the Cleveland Press and the news channels, announced that the Sheraton Hotel was going to be renovated. Well, it was, and then it changed ownership, and the entire concourse was eventually transformed by Forest City Enterprises. As the renovations started some time during my first year of college, I was unaware of what was transpiring in terms of life at The Muffin Basket.

Something strange but not entirely unexpected happened in the lower concourse. Mice starting showing up—everywhere! I had arranged to come back for the summer. Genevieve warned me on the way to my first Saturday back (looking back I realize now that Genevieve kept many things close to the vest, so to speak) that The Muffin Basket had changed. I found out about the mice. Oh my! It was bad. Before we would walk in on Saturday mornings, Genevieve would unlock the door (the owners loved Genevieve and she now had opening responsibilities) and quickly turn on the lights. She said, "Let's wait a minute now." The first time, I said, "Why?" She responded, "We need to give the mice a chance to hide. You don't want to see them all, do you?" Well, I didn't even want to go in, and the donut I had been looking forward to no longer seemed too appetizing. They were everywhere. I went to take a tray down from the top of cabinet and found newborn baby mice on top of it. Oh my gosh—it was so gross. I began making excuses to avoid going to work. The manager was not happy with me and Genevieve told me so. So I bucked up and went, but I was not happy about it.

They weren't doing all the cleaning they used to do. One day I went to start sweeping the floor and as I was getting ready to go under the counter, Genevieve said, "Amzy, you don't want to sweep under there." I was like, "Okay." It bothered me that the standard of cleaning had deteriorated due to the mice. But not doing it then made perfect sense. What if a customer saw them come out?

Life at The Muffin Basket got very complicated. I felt bad for Genevieve. I was able to leave after the summer, and in my heart I knew I was never going to return. I asked Genevieve several months later what was going on and she told me that they were going to shut it down because the whole terminal was going to undergo a transformation. Well, it ended up taking a few more years for that to happen, and my younger sister Isabelle actually was able to work there a couple years. She asked me to sub in for her a few Saturdays one summer. I said I would. But of the four Saturdays she wanted me there, I only came three and was late twice. Phyllis was not happy and Isabelle was very angry with me. I never should have said I would do it because my heart just wasn't in it. The amount of money for the trouble wasn't worth it either. I said I would for my sister, and that was it. I had become the freaky older sister. I guess I deserved it at the time.

The Muffin Basket is no longer in the terminal today. Ironically the area right above where the rats once resided is the indoor location of upscale shops, a restaurant food concourse, and beautiful fountains. A three-story glass wall overlooks the Cuyahoga River. I remember hearing some news about the rat infestation and what a problem it was to eradicate them. I bet they never did.

Again, I need to disclose still more of my life from the Denison house. Mom was not the best dad. She was an improvement over Dad because she didn't strap us, but then again I think she realized that corporal punishment wasn't the right way to teach us a lesson, so to speak. Sammy was having all kinds of problems with school. He never received really good grades. Dad used to punish him when he came home with bad ones—I am pretty sure a strapping was part of the punishment. He never really got the kind of help he needed to learn how to learn (any more than we girls did). Mom and Dad had somehow gotten him into a private high school, but his grades and attendance problems got him expelled. Mom had him go to the dreaded public high school, West Tech I think it was called. All the bad neighborhood boys went to school there. We hoped he wouldn't end up with them, but eventually he did. Mike Cotter was one of the ring leaders. Sammy originally steered clear of him, but later made friends with him because he had no choice. We suspected Sammy was doing drugs. At times he came home with glassy eyes, giggled at things that weren't funny, and was evasive with Mom about his whereabouts. It was like he lived in his own world.

Before long it seemed like Mom had had it with him. I think she was scared of him because a couple times he hit her when they argued. Not like Dad, but still, he should never have touched Mom. Mom had been tough, though. She hit him right back and sent him to his room. One time, though, he left the house. She hollered after him that if he was going to leave, he shouldn't come back. He was gone for several months. Mom got lucky: a friend told Mom where Sammy was and Mom went out and found him and brought him home. Sammy slept and peed for days. I think he was going through drug withdrawal of some kind. I was worried and afraid for him. Then the worst happened.

We lived on a very busy commercial avenue. Traffic noises were loud and especially noticeable at night when I was trying to go to sleep. I personally liked the bedrooms at the back of the house better because they were quieter. One night we saw flashing lights and heard what sounded like screeching brakes. Sammy came running into the house and begged Mom to hide him. In an instant police were at the door. Mom recently recounted this incident to me. She said, "Amzy, the police saw Sammy run toward the house and came to the door right behind him. He barely had a chance to talk to me. They wanted to arrest him and take him. I tried to argue with them not to, but they wouldn't listen to me. I tried to tell them that he said he did not steal the car, it was some other boys. The policemen wouldn't listen and they handcuffed him and took him away." We asked Mom what happened. She said Sammy had been with boys who stole a car. They were just turning onto Denison when the police caught them. The boys jumped out and ran in all directions, but Sammy got caught. He had no place to run because they stopped the car right in front of our house. Sammy had to go with the police to help round up the other boys that were involved. Mom later informed us, "Sammy said he didn't take anything, but he was with them."

For some unknown reason, I felt I needed to discuss Mom's rendition of this timeframe with Sammy. So I called him and here is what he said: "Amzy, tell the truth, I helped steal that car." I quietly listened to his story and didn't divulge that Mom hadn't told us girls the truth all those years ago; she probably wanted us to understand that Sammy had a problem, but that in his heart he really didn't want to do the wrong thing. So she masked the truth. "Sammy," I asked, "What happened with the court? Is that why you went to juvenile hall?" "No, Amzy, I was categorized as "unruly," and Fr. John counseled Mom that it would be best to have me sent to a juvenile correction facility as a minor. I was seventeen. He and Mom decided I might have a chance at a better life if the correction facility worked with me and was able to turn me around before I got in serious trouble at eighteen. Fr. John and Mom did the right thing."

"Sammy," I asked, "Why did Dad always hit you and Faith with the strap? The two of you always seemed to get it when there was a fight." "Amzy, Dad was abusive. He just hit us and didn't know how to parent. I think this is how he was brought up. He didn't know what to do to get us to change our behaviors other than strap us." "Sammy, do you see a correlation between Dad's parenting and your behavior as a teen?" "Absolutely. Dad was detached. When he was told about my behavior, he became quite graphic in terms of what would happen to me if I went to jail. He didn't know how to help me, just tell me what would happen. He never did anything to change my life or any of ours. He didn't know how or he didn't want to." When I heard him say this, tears started welling in my eyes.

Another aspect of Sammy's adolescent behavior was scary, and he unintentionally reminded me about it while we talked. "Amzy, I was always running. Remember the time I left with some friends and Mom had to come and get me in West Virginia? I just didn't want to stay around any more, and a friend said he was going to West Virginia, and I went with him. Mom ended up finding out where I was from one of the people we met along the way who casually asked for my telephone number, and used it to call Mom. I was always running from something. Most of the time, there was really no reason to. I just thought there was and I stopped facing up to my responsibilities. Running was easier."

I don't know how much the court heard of Sammy's delinquency problems, but after the car-stealing incident, Sammy was allowed home while he waited for the final directions from the judge. He was so calm and I wished all of this hadn't happened. I think he did too. The court decided to send him to a juvenile correction facility in Southern Ohio. I often wondered why Mom didn't do more to help him. Sammy was the victim. Yes, he shouldn't have gone with those boys and yes, he was stupid. But he helped the police and he said he would never do anything like this again and he didn't. But then again, he never came back to live at home after this either.

"Sammy was lucky," Mom said to us after she returned from his court hearing. "He will be going to a juvenile hall for a year. There he will receive counseling and if he behaves well, he will get released." We all looked forward to the day Sammy would come home and were happy he was going to be away from the bad neighbors. Sammy was afraid that they would be out to get him because he had to snitch on them—one of the guys had threatened to kill him.

Mom was told when she could come and visit Sammy, but she wasn't sure exactly how to go about letting them know she wanted to visit. So when the time came, a few of us went along for the drive, hoping we could see him. Mom said she wasn't sure if we would be allowed to come in. Recently she filled me in on this event. She said, "Remember when we went to visit Sammy the first time? You girls wanted to come with, but when we got there, they wouldn't let you in. They said Sammy tried to run away and he was being confined as a punishment; they wouldn't allow you girls to see him, but they let me. They took away his shoes and socks. I spoke to the man who was counseling him. Sammy's counselor was a good person: He and his family took Sammy in after he was allowed to leave. I was proud of Sammy. He was allowed to come home, but chose not to. He said he was afraid he would fall in again with all those kids and he didn't want to come back. That man and his family took care of Sammy until he was on his own." I asked, "Does Sammy still see those people today, Mom?" She replied, "Yes, as far as I know, he still sees them and is very good friends with them."

I checked in with Sammy about why he tried to run away back then. He chuckled and told me his story. "Amzy, it was spring and rumor had it that during spring someone always tried to run away. One day I was on my way to the infirmary and I looked down at my feet and decided to run. Once I got out to the street, I realized it was stupid and I started walking back. Someone from the facility saw me on the road and reported it. I was picked up and brought back." I asked, "Was there a reason why you ran?" "No," Sammy replied. "The worst thing I had to deal with there was not having any privacy, even in the bathroom. Being from an all-girl family, I had so much privacy, I was shocked by male nudity. I had to sit on a toilet right next to other guys." "Gross," I said. "Yep," he replied.

Then I could hear a voice in the background telling Sammy he should move his truck at the end of the drive near a box or something and unload. "Gotta go, Amzy." "I love you Sammy," I said. He echoed back, "Love you too."

The realization hit me that there was a discrepancy between Sammy and Mom's stories about the car-stealing incident. I decided to investigate and called Mom on it again. "Mom, why did you tell me Sammy didn't steal the car, because he told me otherwise?" Mom queried, "What did he say?" "He said he stole it with the other boys." Mom chuckled a little and said, "The car belonged to one of the boys' dads. When they took the car, the dad called the police and reported it. He never pressed charges." "Mom," I said, "I love Sammy's integrity. He wasn't going to deny his involvement. He owned up to it." "Yes," Mom said, "I love him for it too."

I had a friend problem of my own in the offing and she came with the name of Tammy Tucker. She wasn't my best friend at first. We had been in the same class in second grade, and she had me over to her house once to play. She wanted to play school. I have a vague memory of helping her arrange the fictional classroom with some of the furniture in her basement. Then she called her brother down and she proceeded to pretend she was a teacher. I don't think I liked the game and after a short time was trying to think of a way to change the game or leave. I think Mom called and it was time for me to go home.

Tammy and I didn't really spend any time together again until the sixth grade. Then we started walking to and from school together on a fairly regular basis. I guess sixth grade is one of those years where friends start mattering. We seemed pretty tight. She started inviting me over. Then we seemed off again, as she became more committed to another girl that walked to and from school. Then this girl, I think her name was Lauri, shifted friendships to my friend Cindy. So Tammy and I were on again. Really, I don't think one happened because of the other, but who knows. It was too long ago.

Anyway, Tammy and I gradually became very good friends. When eighth grade came, we were walking home with each other daily. Tammy had developed physically more than me and more than many other girls. She was clearly big-chested, but she was a little heavy so she seemed proportional. Then in our freshman year of high school this changed. She started losing weight, except for the chest. She became boy crazy. Another thing changed. She wanted to cruise around in her car. She got everything. Her grandma had helped her buy her first car. I don't remember what kind it was, but I do remember it was blue. Anyway, cruising around because you just got your license and a new car was fine. But then she added some things to the mix which made me extremely uncomfortable. She wanted to pick up friends and party. Then it was boys too. She really had gone to the loony bin over boys. She was particularly smitten with one boy and would always drive by his house; she really wanted to be his girlfriend. She was persistent and eventually—though I wasn't around to see it—got together with that boy. I guess I wasn't cool enough to hang with while she was managing this. She ended up getting pregnant. She decided to have the baby and didn't even consider an abortion. I don't recall if abortions were legal then. This would have been about 1976.

Tammy was one of those rare people for whom the hardship of having her own child and dropping out of high school was probably a good thing. She finished high school at West Tech by attending summer classes while she was pregnant. She was determined not to be a dropout, and she succeeded. I was impressed by her drive. She moved into an apartment and the baby looked so much like her. The boyfriend ended up being a creep and totally dropped her. She started dating other guys. I didn't see her as often. She got a job at AmeriTrust in some capacity and seemed to be doing well. I hated that she was still into drugs, partially because I knew drugs were bad. But, the fact that she had a good job and seemed to have a comfortable life made me give her more leeway than she deserved—I should have followed my gut reaction and stayed away from drugs.

College and Beyond

I went off to college. Tammy called me once and desperately wanted to visit me at school, but once she arrived, she wanted me to come with her and drive around as she talked. All she did was talk about all her problems. I realized that was all she ever needed me for—to talk about all of her problems.

The summer after my freshman year of college, I got together with her a few times. I told her my freshman roommate was into partying and bought pot all the time on campus. She asked me if I knew who she bought from. I said that lots of people sold it and that I knew a couple. Tammy gave me some pot to take back to college, which she may have made me pay her for. It was weird. Tammy had invited me to smoke a "dooby" several times before going to college, but I had always pretended to inhale and never got high. I partied with my roommate only because she was so persistent and driven to get everyone high. She was hard to say no to. But in reality I never really got high and if I did, I never enjoyed it. I silently sat nearby and watched my roommate enjoy getting everyone she invited over get high.

Anyway, Tammy gave me this pot and I actually liked my high for the first and only time in my life. I think it may have been laced with a narcotic because it took effect very quickly and made me feel different. I decided to share it with a couple guys, who I invited to my dorm room. I couldn't believe it but I got caught. This was the only time I had initiated a party in my life and I got caught. Mom got a letter home from the school and she came and had a long talk with me. My boyfriend at the time was on the student counsel, and he told me he tried to pull the letters home but missed mine. Mom wanted to bring me home for the weekend. I needed a break from campus and agreed to the idea. We had a long talk in the car. She said how bad it is to do drugs and she never really came out and said she got the letter, but of course I knew she had. Mom knew I was smoking marijuana and she thought I should quit. I said, "Okay, Mom." Then she persisted just a little more and said, "Promise." "I promise." I followed through on my oath. A couple of times in the future I made an exception, but each time I was uncomfortable and really didn't enjoy the experience. These occasions were much later. One was in my junior year of college, and the other was post-college during a visit with old college friends.

The new me was somewhat difficult to comprehend at first. But saying no and dealing with drug culture acquaintances was much easier than I anticipated. Around this point in time, a movie had come out about a young girl that got involved with drugs, and people were talking about how addictive and bad street drugs were. Anyway, peer pressure ended up being more of a stereotype than a reality. Perhaps it was my mindset and commitment to fulfill my promise to my mother that prevailed.

So it was strange at first, because people—who knew I partied—called and I had to tell them I quit. The calls stopped coming very quickly. One guy called to find out if I could sell him some stuff just because of what had happened—I never had sold it, but I guess he thought I had. I told him someone he could buy from and hung up. I was surprised by how easy it was to just say no. But I had to find new friends, and this was a good thing. I started to look at what was really important, and that was graduating from college and getting a good job. I wished I had never let Tammy influence me in the first place, and I got a new roommate because my old one was a drug user and huge pothead. In fact I later discovered that one reason I was caught was because they wanted to catch my roommate. They finally did—like a year later. I saw the head RA walking toward the administration building from our dormitory with a red bong. My roommate had always referred to her bong quite fondly as "Big Red." Immediately I knew the RA had accomplished her task. She smiled at me as she walked by. I smiled back. The following summer I went home for a visit with Grandma. She said Tammy called. She asked if I was going to call her. I told her I didn't have her number. Grandma said Tammy's number was on the fridge and I should call her. I took the number and threw it away upstairs where Grandma couldn't see me do it. I never saw or spoke to Tammy again.

I started developing into a young lady who cared a great deal about her appearance and worked on makeup tricks and all kinds of ways to wear affordable clothing that seemed stylish. Life on a college campus challenged me to dress differently because the culture was different than at home, even though home was only a thirty-minute drive to the other side of town. Kids wore "preppy" clothes—an up and coming fashion trend—and the stores carried various options to emulate this look. I purchased khaki pants in two colors—olive and an off-white. For tops I purchased polo shirts and a couple of button-down print blouses. I would rotate outfits but always had on either of these two pairs of pants. That's all I could afford. My bell-bottom days were over.

My new roommate told me the professors liked the students that looked preppy so I had been highly motivated to get my new clothes. I actually snuck wearing a shirt or two of hers on several occasions until I had my own clothes. She acted like she didn't notice; after all she was the one who tutored me about cleaning up my wardrobe. I knew her class schedule and I would take them off and re-hang them in her closet before she would even know I had worn them. It wasn't right, but this helped motivate me to get my own things. My grades started improving and I attributed this to the clothes. My values had been redirected by appearance in a way that was acceptable. Looking right helped me in numerous ways over the years, but as I am aging, I have challenges with my appearance that are impossible. It seems that lack of popularity and an older body and face share a seat these days.

Somehow, without knowing it, I was crawling out of a sewer of doubts I had been struggling with because of our broken house and my parent's broken marriage. These events created huge chasms of insecurity that overcame me as easily as the gargantuan black-shelled bugs that once crawled out of our floor drains. Because my parents had been authoritarian, because they had divorced and been so involved with their own problems and didn't see ours, and because we didn't know when to get help and how to evaluate our needs properly, my values became skewed. Realizing that my longest-running childhood friend was not a good friend after all was only one symptom of how confused I really was, but I didn't know it at the time. All I knew was I needed to create distance between us just as I had by burying the past by pretending it didn't happen. It was simple. I just never really discussed my family much and life moved on. But burying my past showed up someplace else.

The first dream occurred after we moved away from Denison, and I may have been in college. At first I couldn't make sense of why my dreams seemed so dramatic. I would be running away from something, and as I looked behind me, I saw rats as large as people chasing me. I ran faster, but they seemed to be catching up to me and I would wake up rattled and confused. After having similar dreams on other occasions, I started trying to puzzle through what the dreams could mean. I realized that the rats symbolized my fears; some were big, others small; they seemed to build and build until they would almost overtake me, and I would either need to bury my fears or face them. Of course the rats represented the root causes of my problems. I was a bystander and somewhat of a victim. All those years earlier, I had no control over my parents' lives. I was a child that should be seen and not heard, so what could I do to help or understand what was happening? For so long I didn't even realize that my fears mounted because I never had a way of recognizing or talking about what was confusing me. Life's inconsistencies were scurrying about inside me (just like the terminal rats) and building to a point where they wanted to get my attention. I believe that waking up in time to remember these dreams was my subconscious's way of telling me I needed and/or was ready to face them. More importantly I needed to realize that if I didn't cope with my fears, perhaps they would overtake me in the end. Rats would factor in my dreams for several years to come.

Should I tell more about friend or boy problems? I'll start with friends. I alluded to this issue earlier when I was showing you my father's pictures. Now it seems to me it was easier making friends when we were younger than it is today.

I presently live in an affluent neighborhood. My neighbors sport luxury homes and cars, and take lavish vacations. My husband has done well in his career, so we enjoy many of these material things. Many of these people are gossips and arrogant, and it is difficult to ferret out who is telling the truth and who is digging for dirt. They probably think I am a snob because I don't share their appreciation of trash talk and material things. Who has more is not important to me, so life is very difficult because they exclude you if they don't like something you say or do—or don't do—regarding their standards. You become an outcast. It is a sick neighborhood. I have been a victim of people's invalid estimations of my character, and it really hurts. I don't know if I can do anything to change their judgments about me, so I am trying to just exist without them knowing how badly I believe they act toward me. My kids have all gotten by fine, thank God.

Here is a story about how life can be. My daughter, Sarah, was supposed to have a Halloween outing with a close friend. They planned to dress in the same costumes a year earlier and I thought it was very cute. A third friend was somewhat excluded but not intentionally. Her parents simply would not allow her to choose her costume or her outing so far in advance, so Sarah and Michelle continued periodically talking openly about their plan throughout the year. Every once in awhile, one or the other of them would bring up Halloween, and they would both still agree they were going to dress the same and spend it together. Life was good.

The next school year started and we were carpooling with another neighbor's girl from time to time. I'll name her Theresa. Theresa asked what Sarah was doing for Halloween and Sarah told her. Theresa politely asked if she could join her and Michelle for trick-or-treating. Sarah didn't respond right away, but then said she had planned to do this with Michelle.

A couple weeks later, Theresa asked again. I thought Sarah should have said, "We'll see what we can work out," but since the kids were at an age where they were just starting to figure out how to make their own choices, I thought I would try to stay out of it. Well, I was wrong. Theresa's mom stopped me one day and said, "Why can't Theresa trick-or-treat with Sarah and Michelle?" Before I could reply, she said, "Amzy, I am going to talk to Monica (Michelle's mom) and guess what: I am going to take Monica away from you." I was struck by how childish she sounded and didn't take her too seriously.

But, Monica started berating me when I called to find out what was going on and it soon became clear, she was taking sides. I tried to explain to Monica that the girls had planned everything; that I tried to lend my support and let them direct how they wanted to spend Halloween, but she wouldn't listen. I was deeply hurt by the fact that she wouldn't listen to me. I thought she was a friend who would stand by me and help me out in a pinch, which this situation obviously was, but I was wrong. She abandoned me and our friendship. I was crushed and still am. Dolores, Theresa's mom, probably understood Monica better than I did, but she inadvertently helped me learn something about her and Monica. Monica was and probably always will be concerned only for her girl. She wanted all the girls to come to her house, which was a huge boost for Michelle's social self-esteem, but came at the expense of Sarah's. They had no regard for how Sarah would perceive the change in plans, and of course she was not happy. I had all I could do to explain to Sarah that plans changed and that it had nothing to do with her, but we were inviting more girls to participate in trick-or-treating at Michelle's.

I managed to keep Sarah included in the Halloween outing by explaining to two other moms what had happened and that I would love it if their girls would join in. I explained that the outing would start at Monica's and end in our neighborhood. They grabbed the invitation and did everything they could to make sure Sarah was included by their girls during the outing. Fortunately, it worked out. The weird thing was that all Monica had to do was call me and say, "Amzy, I want to invite more kids in for Halloween. Would you have a problem with that since Michelle had originally planned with Sarah only?" But this was not what occurred, and I know it was because Dolores spoke ill of me. I call her Dolores B to this day. You can figure out what the B stands for. Monica and Dolores B go out of their way to create groups for anything that's happening but exclude Sarah. They continue to rub salt into a wound they created, and I can't do a damn thing about it except let them.

Today, the same moms that came to my rescue then remain aware of the strained relationships and are politely aloof. Recently one of them made sure Sarah got a ride home with a neighbor from an after-school affair. Sarah's dad was to pick her up when it ended. I had to leave her and was politely making sure she had a parent that she could go to in case things ended early or something unforeseen happened. Monica was there when I brought up my situation, and when I asked if anyone could make sure Sarah got her ride with her father, she said, "I can't help you; I need to leave." I could tell from her demeanor and tone of voice, however, that she only said this because she still felt slighted by me. We are more alike than I care to admit. Neither of us liked what had happened that Halloween, but she would never apologize for handling it the way she did and, of course, I don't believe I need to either. So the incident, our feelings, and our relationship remain unresolved.

As far as helpful moms go, they acted like true friends. I am very unhappy about the situation with Monica (and Dolores B). I worry about Monica because of Dolores B, but I stay away from both of them because they don't seem to be able to recognize that my and Sarah's personhood matter just as much as theirs. I am still climbing out of this sewer.

One thing that was difficult for me to figure out growing up was relationships with boys. I was on homecoming court for high school, the ugly duckling turned into a swan, and I was picked to represent my school for St. Edward's Homecoming. St. Edward is a private school for boys in Lakewood, Ohio. It is actually only a couple miles from our old Lakewood home, but at that time we lived on West Boulevard (on the border of Lakewood, but still in Cleveland proper). We had moved from the Denison house and rented half of a duplex. I liked this house. By this time the only siblings left with Mom were Genevieve, Isabelle, Tristen, and me (and Faith for a short time). It was 1977. I was a senior.

As a result of going out for court, some of the boys at St. Edward started to learn about me. A few of them wanted to date me. Boys wanted to date girls then and girls wanted to be asked out. I was high on the list of desirables because I had been on court. My cousin was a senior at St. Edward so this helped. The boys would ask who I was dating. One guy in particular wanted to date me and Cousin Tom was quite impressed and seemingly excited about the match. His name was Ken James. When Tom told me I said, "Okay Tom, what do you think of this guy?" He replied, "Oh, he's a really good guy, Amzy. He is captain of the hockey team and a lot of people like him." I said, "Okay, I'll go out with him." So Tom gave him my number and he called and we agreed to meet. I don't remember the exact way we first met. I think we arranged to come to a party at one of Ken's friend's homes. So Tom picked me up along with another friend or two and we went. Ken went out of his way to say hello and hang out with me awhile during the party. He was very handsome. I thought, "Well, that's that." But then he called me to go out again. He wanted me to come to one of his hockey games. I went. Next I was invited to his house. I thought he must really like me until after we double-dated with his older brother. At the end of the date, he walked me to the door and gave me our first kiss, and it was perfect. He lingered and leaned into me (perhaps in part due to the fact that he was on crutches from a recent hockey injury), which heightened the affect his kiss had on me. Our first kiss was the only one. He never called me after that.

Recently I had a dream about Ken. He was very serious about me. We seemed to be at some resort and we were lying in bed kissing. He had initiated the encounter. We did not do anything else—just held each other and kissed. The experience of kissing him was so wonderful when it finally had first happened to me in real life, I was easily able to relive the experience in my dreams and expand it somewhat. Anyway, after we kissed he told me something was bothering him about how people wanted him to act and he wasn't sure what to do. It was like he was inviting me to say something because he paused before he went on. I didn't say anything and waited for him to continue. Reflecting back on the dreamscape, I now realize that all those years ago Ken had made a decision to act the way others wanted him to, to make everything okay. It hit me that he and I could never have been together, because he could act and I couldn't. It also hit me that he may even have alluded to the fact that he wasn't going to see me anymore, and I either didn't accept it or didn't put two and two together. In my dream I broke up with him, but in reality he broke up with me. I couldn't relive the same outcome in my dream that had puzzled and distressed me so long in real life. Everything was perfect. Why did he stop seeing me? He was destined for a great career and became an attorney. My life took a different path. I guess, deep down, I have known all these years that he could adapt to people and situations that I struggled with then and still do now. It took me all these years and a dream to understand why he had stopped dating me (other than perhaps his brother or his best friend—whose name I don't recall—didn't like either me or how I looked or a combination of both).

The boy thing didn't get easier for a long time. I dated several guys in and after college. It wasn't until I was twenty-six that Mr. Right came along. We married two years later and last May celebrated our twenty-second anniversary. We have had everything together—passionate kisses, feisty fights, wonderful children, and a life filled with more than I could have ever imagined. God blessed me, regardless of my seeming inability to get it right.

As time moved forward, the distance between me and the Denison house increased in direct proportion to how much I needed to bury the memories and embarrassment of coming from a broken family, once on welfare, and fighting every moment of our lives to change all the bad things that happened there into something worth living for. More than poor judgment about drugs and friends had crept into my life, but having experienced the downside of making poor choices, I was determined not to make these mistakes again. I did not want to end up in jail and absolutely wanted to make a better life for myself than my parents had. I drove myself harder than ever to look for ways to improve my outlook, my grades, and my future. I had many more life lessons ahead of me to learn, but I definitely was headed in the right direction.

As college progressed some good things started happening. I wasn't living at home and I determined I would reside on campus all four years of school, mostly because I couldn't afford otherwise. Residing on campus rather than at home gave me freedom and independence, and even though it scared me at first, I was growing to like it; and I felt safe. Ironically, because our family was low income, I qualified for enough financial aid to cover room and board. After my sophomore year of school, my roommate and many classmates planned to move off campus—those who had parents who helped pay their rent. I was not one of them and tried to make it seem like I simply preferred to live on campus because it was more convenient. (I am sure several of these kids realized I couldn't afford to do otherwise even if I wanted to.) However, I had determined that this would also be better because I couldn't afford a car to travel to and from campus. Walking ten minutes from the dorm to the classrooms was ideal. My grades started improving because I got rid of my druggy roommate and started having positive experiences, such as study groups and trips to the mall. I started working a part-time job with a local bank in branch operations. This gave me some spending money for clothing and personal necessities.

Day-to-day life on campus was exciting in so many ways. I became acquainted with many kids from the area and from far away, including those attending from coast to coast. There was a guy from California; a couple guys from Mexico; girls and guys from Michigan, Illinois, and Indiana—basically from the nearby Midwest states—and local kids.

One guy in particular, from Maine, took an interest in me. He was a great guy, but he demanded too many favors from our budding friendship. I liked him because he was smart, witty, and a frat leader of sorts. I'll call him "The Boyfriend." The first time he invited me to his room I was a little nervous about it. His invitation was so genuine. He stopped by my table in the library and said hello. I had seen him in the cafeteria, and then my roommate had mentioned his name and we became acquainted, but I don't really remember who introduced us. One day, after a group of us had been complaining about the food in the cafeteria, he went out of his way to walk with me back from the library and invited me to his room, saying, "Amzy, why don't you come over and I'll make you a steak dinner?" He was very matter-of-fact and seemed to be making a genuinely friendly gesture. Let me tell you, the best way to a young girl's heart is through her stomach. His cooking was so good.

He made moves on me that same night and almost every night we spent together afterwards. I thought he was it. He once quoted Robert Frost's poem "The Road Not Taken" when we were together and he was in one of his philosophical moods. He was very serious about what he wanted to do with his life after college and believed he was going to take a path most people didn't travel. He was very subtle, and part of me felt he was hinting that we were not destined to be together. I missed his reason for dating me, even when he played me one of his favorite songs, Bread's "Baby I'm-A Want You." The lyrics tell of a guy who is dating a girl and realizes she is not in love with him. At least this was and still is my interpretation. As I look back and remember our relationship, I realize the irony in those lyrics.

The Boyfriend ended up being elusively deceitful, but probably felt he was justified. He thought a lot about himself and how smart he was. The Boyfriend graduated with honors and went on for a master's degree in Washington in the field of psychology. I continued our relationship until I hadn't heard from him for awhile and concluded he didn't want to see me anymore. Then all of a sudden one or another of his old frat brothers would happen by and say, "I talked to The Boyfriend, and he says hello." I guess The Boyfriend started to realize I needed some assurances about his affection for me. Or perhaps those brothers did. Then others were telling me that long-distance romances don't last. I knew they heard from The Boyfriend and I thought this was their way of telling me he had moved on. When people asked me how The Boyfriend was, for awhile I said, "Fine."

Then I started to be honest and say, "I don't know, I haven't talked to him for awhile." Then he would call and I would think life was normal again, except I had no one to see during free time on campus.

I started thinking about seeing other guys. I had had my eye on one for quite some time, and he ended up asking me over for a party. The Boyfriend heard about it and suddenly came for a visit. Shortly after his announced arrival (by some of his frat brothers with the warning he was mad at me), he came to see me in my dorm room and demanded me to explain why I was seeing other guys. I apologetically explained to him that I didn't think he was interested in me anymore, and he was angry. I told him I would stop. He seemed okay with this, and life moved on. I continued to see him and talk to him on the phone sporadically, but our conversations always sounded the same. We had nothing new to say to each other, which indicated to me he had moved on; but he never told me this, and it took me the balance of my senior year and another year before the relationship officially ended.

In the meantime he explained that his lack of attentiveness to me was due to the fact that he had so much work. I decided he was a workaholic, so I could understand the lack of communication and genuine lack of interest in my life. Then one day I called him up and he finally told me that he was breaking up with me—over the phone. He was probably going to break up with me that day in the dormitory when he confronted me about dating another guy but decided not to when I apologized to him. Thinking back on his nature, I think he made me a pawn in his game. It has taken me time to put it all in perspective. Back then, to be told over the phone that he was breaking up with me was very upsetting. I cried for a long time. I happened to be at home when the phone break-up occurred, and Genevieve was beside herself seeing me the way I was. She asked me for his phone number, called him, told him what a jerk he was (along with a few other expletives), and then hung up.

He led me to believe that he had accepted my apologies, but he hadn't. It took me a long time to get over him, even though he handled everything like a creep. I have to say I probably deserved some of this treatment. This relationship taught me to be honest with people about my feelings even if I think it might hurt them. I was afraid to tell him I wanted to date other guys and not him alone, and I went ahead with dating without closure on our relationship. I was afraid he would be mean to me somehow. He had been physically mean to me once before and I didn't want it to happen again.

The central irony about sex is that it's bad fun and adds an element of adventure to life not only by virtue of the fact that there are opposites, male and female, but we each have a unique combination of opposites (from what I observe and hear from others) and we share this with another (or others if you're ultra-liberal.) I am a textbook heterosexual female. Okay, this is not unique. But what I bring to a sexual encounter by virtue of being different intellectually and emotionally from any other female (and any other male for that matter) makes my sexual adventure unique. Add to this that my partner(s) is/(are) determined from those people I encounter in life and of those, the one(s) whom I choose to be with. My sexual adventure is totally unique.

A person doesn't fully understand what sex is or what it means until he/she encounters it with another. It's obvious people love having sex because the fallen risk being caught in extra-marital affairs and contracting sexual diseases. Society gets carried away with it.

Ironically, my generation's parents didn't communicate to us enough about it. Most teenagers were simply ignorant of the consequences of a sexual encounter and teenagers were and are innately reckless to begin with, simply because of having these wonderfully youthful bodies that are completely developed before emotions and intelligence mature. Add to this that our commercial society has separated the sacred part of sexual intimacy from the sex act—and guess what? Sex becomes an enticing act that needs to be experienced. It took a few falls for me to realize that it deserved to be much more than this.

The Boyfriend erred here too. I was stranded in the car with him after he dropped off a drunken friend of mine who couldn't give us proper directions to her home. He didn't like that he had to drive so long and we got lost. He took his anger out on me by pulling over to the side of the road in a remote area after dropping her off, grabbing me by the back of the neck, pulling me toward his exposed genitals, which he had quickly maneuvered out of his unzipped pants, and forcing me to perform oral sex until he came. I thought I deserved it for being so stupid about the directions. I tried to break free but couldn't because he was so strong. What I was stupid about was not ending the relationship right then and there. I was such an insecure person.

The Boyfriend only called when he thought I was cheating or didn't need him. He was immature and had gradually become disinterested in me as a person. He (and his frat brothers) had this attitude that I was his sex property: I was the girlfriend who would visit him whenever he needed. So once he graduated and moved on, his ties to the college frat consisted of his intentions to monitor me and to serve in an alumni capacity to fulfill his frat obligations, playing the role of prestigious alumni to lure in a pledge base, thus sustaining the fraternity for the future. By the end of my senior year, I barely saw him and I don't recall how often we spoke on the phone. I am sure it varied—sometimes once a week; sometimes once a month. I kept hoping that The Boyfriend still cared. I ignored my instincts, which were telling me it was over. I had buried my fears yet again.

My parents had never explained to me how to deal with difficult or abusive people. On the contrary, abuse seemed normal in my life due to my sibling fights and disgruntled, arguing parents. I witnessed them growing up abusing each other, so I didn't even realize how wrong it was for this guy to do what he did to me. That's the part of the abuse cycle which society needs to break. Educate kids from broken families even if they say they aren't having a problem with fighting at home. They may be too embarrassed to admit it or they may not even know it's not normal. Find a way to get involved, but helpfully involved.

It took conversations with friends for me to realize this guy was a creep, but it took *me* to listen to their message, and unfortunately I listened too late. It's important that you point out to people in this situation that for some reason they may not be thinking clearly about the relationship. I certainly wasn't. I wanted one boyfriend at a time because I didn't want people to think I would go around with just any guy. But when it wasn't right, I couldn't recognize it.

I have come to believe that part of the reason I couldn't see it—that is, what the consequences would mean to me relative to my sexual relations—was linked to the fact that I was a child of the "sexual revolution," which meant you could have sex with anyone, any time. My generation got caught up in the Sixties' revolution at a time when our parents were coping with traditional norms about raising children. Free sex was like free candy, yours for the taking. Of course we would discover that sexual freedom brought consequences —and not just the toll sexual freedom took in the form of misguiding my generation's values. These relationships resulted in a soaring number of abortions, an ever increasing climb in the divorce rate, and the rapid spread of new and old types of sexual diseases, including AIDS. My adolescent generation barely escaped this disease. We were fortunate…Now I need to get back to my life…

I don't know why The Boyfriend was upset by me dating other guys other than the fact that he assumed I would also be sexually active with them too. The sexual revolution had distorted our values and caused everyone to assume things about people who liked each other. In four words: we were all confused. He was mad because he assumed I ended the relationship and he wanted to get even, only he wouldn't tell me. He wasn't entirely wrong about me. I had gone to a party another guy invited me to. I knew the other guy liked me and I liked him, but I didn't consider it a date. It was a party. I ended up having too much to drink and slept there. I don't know what the guy told The Boyfriend or his frat brothers, but I am sure the truth was distorted to make me appear the villain. I learned a lot about guys and how they are. I decided never to travel alone with a guy unless I felt comfortable with him, and I would sometimes take my girl friends along, and even then choose shorter outings to public places where I was less likely to be vulnerable.

Standard marriage vows do not clearly address chastity (this is a value derived from biblical interpretations and is somehow understood by society to be important for the sanctity and success of each marriage). So my fiancé, Charles, and I saw the importance of discussing this and creating a pact before we married: our marriage would be over if either one of us would have sexual relations with others. I have held up my end of the bargain and I know Charles has too. It's tough to ignore certain feelings for other people, but it keeps our marriage strong to have this joint assurance. It is one of the most important aspects of married life. One cannot betray it and I hope I never do. But how could I explain to The Boyfriend that he had misunderstood the situation when I didn't know what he had been told. More importantly I didn't have a firm understanding myself about the differences in the levels of relationships, both in terms of values and how to properly handle things when my values were challenged. I had nobody teach me how to understand what a healthy relationship was; but somehow I knew the one I had with The Boyfriend was not right. I just didn't know how to handle it. I was totally immature.

My parents never explained relationships to me. Grandma Romauch told me post-college that guys like bad girls a lot, but they don't marry them. Grandma Braun taught me—again post-college—how guys really like you if you aren't easy, but it took me a long time to understand what that meant. It didn't mean in a sexual way but too easy to be with. Guys like hard-to-get.

Once I figured this out, I gave up trying to flirt with guys and most certainly stopped any inclination toward what could be construed as chasing after them. I changed my outlook on life to set professional goals and strive for personal achievement. I certainly wished I had learned this lesson much earlier in life. So...I share it here. A woman needs to be true to herself first. If you are too serious or chase guys or are too easy—either sexually or in terms of accessibility—guys will have no respect for you. A woman cannot put aside her personhood for a guy. They ultimately don't understand it. I guess what I am trying to explain is, don't sacrifice your values, and if a guy wants you to, he's not worth it. Make sure you learn that your values, including that of good friendship, must be fostered first in any relationship. If a friend doesn't want to talk to you or spend time with you, he or she is not a friend. It's weird, but that's how it works. You are ready to marry or have a meaningful relationship when you are both fully committed. It must be clearly communicated and understood by both parties. Both parties cannot be confused by geographic boundaries or hidden secrets or whatever else can cause misunderstandings about the other; and if they are, those discrepancies need to be resolved for true unity to continue.

Life moved on and I graduated from college. Dad and Mom were both in attendance on the big day. The Boyfriend was not there. I was so nervous about both parents sharing the same space, but it worked. Dad took a picture of me in cap and gown and I still have the photo. I was worried he was going to hit on Mom and get sappy like he had on so many other occasions after their divorce. For a long time, when he came over to pick us up for visitation, he took the opportunity to beg Mom to take him back and tell her how much he loved her. Mom was steadfast, though. It was over and there was no going back. Over time I guess Dad gave up, but I wasn't around to see the change. On my graduation day, I thought it could still happen, but it didn't. That was the first time I had them together in one space, and it was all about me. It was a little weird, but like I said, it worked. I wish now that we had shared more times like this. My thoughts shift to my husband's parents, who are also divorced. I realize how lucky he is to have them both and that they care so much about us and their grandchildren. It's like they are the parents I never had, and even though they're divorced and it's difficult for them to share the same space, we have a family dynamic that allows us to grieve together for the bad and work it out for the good. Today it would be said that we are dysfunctional and to this I say, "What family isn't?"

I met Charles when I was twenty-six, and we married two years later. Charles got to meet Dad, and Dad liked him. Everyone in my family liked Charles. For some reason this surprised me. I expected more opposition to

Charles because family members often disagreed about my choices. There was none. Every time some member of the family met Charles, he or she came away liking him. I was happy about this. The only bump we had while we were dating proved to be an opportunity for me to get to know this guy even better. Grandma Braun coached me through the bump in the road. We were supposed to go out either for the fifth or sixth time. He had been pretty specific about it, but, he didn't call to firm it up, leaving me wondering if we were still on. I told Grandma and she said, "You need to call him on it." I thought she meant tell him that he shouldn't have done it, but as I sat there, she clarified, "Amzy, this is a time you should call him right away and talk to him about it." She wanted me to literally call him right at that moment. It dawned on me that I should try out her advice. I hesitated and then thought to myself, "I am afraid he won't care, but what have I got to lose." I echoed my thought out loud, and Grandma told me in a firm voice, "Call." I got up and called him. Grandma listened in the whole time. When I got off the phone, she said, "Amzy, you said all the right things. Now let's wait and see what happens. I bet you're going to be surprised." She was right! About a half hour later, Charles was at the door with a dozen roses, asking to visit with me. I was shocked and had a new respect for Grandma. I got a dozen roses and Charles out of just "calling him on it." What a valuable lesson! I knew then he was Mr. Right.

After we married I was always struck by how tender and loving he was even after some of the major fights we had. He cared so deeply about me and still does today. We have been through so much together, and we've somehow held on to each other. I think it was a year or two after our marriage, and we were on our third of many moves in our lives together, when I had a dream about rats again. But something interesting happened in the dream. I was running away from them, but then I stopped. They stopped right in front of me and nothing happened. The dream ended and I woke up and I haven't had a dream about rats since. Charles saved me somehow. God, I am so lucky you gave me Charles.

Before I end my story, I need to back up just a tad and share my career challenges and setbacks, because it is within the search for my own path that I discovered a kinship with Dad and a shared a common tie with Mom.

While in college I discovered that I was not capable of thinking on an analytical level necessary to pursue the business degree I had dreamed of. I wanted to be the success Uncle Jake had been and so I gained admission to the same university. As I would soon discover, it wasn't easy. I couldn't readily comprehend the business concepts presented. I realized a little too late that I needed to improve my study and reading comprehension skills.

In high school I never had to crack a book and became familiar with the text more from listening to lectures. I discovered that my high school teachers presented very accurate and articulate descriptions of the text so I rarely had to take notes and simply inhaled the rest. I always did my projects and homework assignments in a timely fashion and came away with a respectable grade point average of 3.33.

In college this was not enough. In lectures professors often went off on tangents that were over my head. I found reading the text was an absolute necessity, but I had difficulty managing my time so I could sit down and do it with a modicum of uninterrupted privacy. I soon found that getting into the business school was going to be a wish and a prayer.

During winter break my sophomore year of college, while family had gone to visit my aunt and uncle, I reclined on the sofa at Grandma's, looked at the Christmas tree lights, and began crying. It was more than a cry: I sobbed. What was I going to do? At first my body gave into the watery cleansing of my spirit, but as my sobs turned into that dry heaving of emptiness that usually follows a good cry, I suddenly felt a surge of anger that oddly strengthened my resolve to finish college—somehow. Then, I thought: "I am the only one who can figure this out. What can I do and do well? What has been causing me to be unsuccessful?" I answered the thought with, "I know I can read and I know I can learn to write." Armed with this self-awareness, I then thought, "What major would help me enjoy my college experience and allow me to expand these abilities?" Well, I couldn't become a communications major because I didn't want to get anywhere near my former roommate, whom I knew was pursuing this course, so English popped into my head. English became my major and I soon declared it upon my return to school. I flourished with this newly found focus. I studied Shakespeare, eighteenth-century British literature, American literature, Chaucer, drama, and literary criticism. I truly came away with a wonderful backdrop for literary success, but as I approached my senior year I still wanted to somehow work my talents into the business world. This was the only place I could be a success like my uncle. I was so wrong.

I look back today and wonder what people thought about me and what they thought they could do with me when I interviewed. It was a different time in America. I graduated in 1982. It was an inflationary period, with low entry wages for common college graduates. Since I had worked part time in branch operations for Society National Bank, I decided to interview for a full-time position in the home office, which was closer to home and on the bus line in terms of a commute. The branch posted internal openings and after indicating my interest to the customer service representative, CR for short (which was a well-respected position in a branch), she directed me toward one or two postings. A trust position seemed the most promising. I went into the city and interviewed with someone in human resources, and he seemed to like me. But after several weeks of not hearing any news, I asked the CR what I should do. She told me to call human resources and follow up. So I did. A week later the CR called me over to her desk and told me she had good news: they wanted to offer me the job. The job was described to me in more detail, and the duties seemed too easy—I was going to be some kind of glorified file clerk. She told me the job paid "eleven," which was considered a very respectable starting salary. I thought eleven dollars an hour would be great! Time passed and I started telling classmates I had a job at graduation in the trust department that would pay about twenty grand a year. I remember getting a lot of oohs and aahs.

The first day was great, and again I thought the job was too easy. Then I thought, "They are going easy on me because I just started." After I learned the job, I remarked to the department supervisor that I was wondering what else I should be doing, because the job seemed so easy. She said, "It is an easy job; just do it the best way you can, Amzy." "Wow, that's weird," I thought. Then my first paycheck came and I discovered that the job paid eleven grand a year, not eleven dollars an hour. If anyone saw my face when the realization came, they would have seen my embarrassment, confusion, and disbelief. Well, the mistake had been mine and it took me four or five years of attempts to improve my career path within the bank—and a later realization that I never would—for me to start making plans to pursue a different pathway toward success.

This was the second crossroad I had arrived at in life—after the one about choosing my college major. I redefined my priorities first. At the top of my list was becoming more financially independent. I still lived with Grandma, and I really wanted to move out and be on my own. I tried to determine what my salary needed to be to afford apartment living. I just needed to bump it up about five grand. I started looking at postings in terms of salary and not in terms of career path. Secretarial jobs all paid what I needed to earn. I thought that was ironic. I remember thinking, "God, I never wanted to be like my Mom, but what choice do I have?" So I pursued secretarial course work with a school called Bryant and Stratton. A little over a year later, I had transformed myself into a secretary and was quickly given a job in the mortgage department with an appraiser. Well, it allowed me to easily pay off my college loan and have money left over. I bought my first car, a large, brown Ford sedan. It was in great condition and I loved driving to work, but it meant I had to pay for parking daily, which was more than the cost of a bus ride. So I alternated between driving and riding the bus, depending on my after-work and morning schedules.

This position wasn't getting me anywhere. An old college associate—I'll call her Bridgette—also worked in branch operations and was promoted to a management trainee position; I couldn't figure out why, especially because I had a year seniority on her. I called the CR and chitchatted and then politely brought up the subject. She said, "Amzy, Bridgette got that job because she majored in finance and they wanted business majors for trainee positions. They would never place you in a position like that." Boy, what a slap in the face her remark was. I regretted more than ever being me.

I retaliated by starting a job search outside of the bank. About three months later, I was offered a job with a law firm, which lured me away with a salary four grand more than I was currently making, a health plan, and pension benefits. I found it very easy to leave.

Long story short, two years later I discovered secretarial work wasn't for me, and I pursued paralegal work. I landed a job with a large mining company that paid for my paralegal certification, and even though I only stayed with this company a couple years, I found subsequent positions as a paralegal in various fields of law and with various companies and law firms. I stopped working only after Charles got a huge promotion and salary boost. I reprioritized my life again, and knowing it was long overdue for me to give more attention to my son, I shifted my career to focus on my son's life, planning for a second child, and managing the household.

I had successfully inched my way up to paralegal, but not head paralegal on any team over a period of eleven years. I didn't feel like much of a success and pursued parenthood with zest to make up for my seeming lack of perfection. I look back now and realize that even though I had many embarrassments as well as career lows, I had some good moments too. I joined a young professionals group where I met my future husband, Charles; I discovered a true enjoyment of real estate law and its methodical dedication with isolating, defining, and establishing property ownership; I became a devoted mother to my son and later, my daughter; and I began understanding life better because I managed to sustain myself with successes somehow gifted to me in spite of myself and my failings.

I realize today that I will never go back to paralegal work if I can help it. I attained a respectable salary level, which never would have been achieved if I had remained a bank clerk or a secretary; but working with attorneys that were perhaps more psychotic about perfection than I was had its pluses and minuses. The big pluses: I learned how to research and it is now a pleasure for me; I learned how to approach writing and now it is my first love; I worked with great people, some of the best I think life has to offer (which I know is debatable when it comes to attorneys); and I realized that I could provide service professionally in a team environment. These are things I carry and share from my whole being, and which I know have been appreciated and rewarded. But one thing paralegal work never gave me was equality with attorneys. I realize now that attorneys take oaths and as such have much more on the line in terms of their client responsibilities. But I felt responsible for doing my job to the best of my ability, and I wondered, "Why shouldn't I be thought of as a professional?" I got carried away with semantics. But it's true that paralegals have their own professional ghetto, which is the only way I can describe it. It was that metaphorical hell I shared with Dad. I got out of it and never wish to go back.

A couple years ago, I started dabbling with poetry. I produced musings in a free form style that I had come across when studying Wallace Stevens in college. None of my poetry has been published, but I am blessed that I could discover this part of my nature. It has helped me realize that true success comes from within. Even if I am the only one reading my work, as long as I can look at each poem, enjoy it, and rediscover the meaning with a smile and heartfelt understanding each time, I know it's a part of me that someone else may also enjoy someday. About a year into this new venture, I went to sleep one night and had a dream. I remembered most of it upon waking and wrote down what I saw into the following words. My poem is merely a written remembrance of my dream:

Dream Poem

The incredible, muscular, sleek, black stallion

Appeared out of nowhere

He stood and swayed to help his passengers on

Donning an orange, red, rustic wool blanket and an enormous saddle

The stallion was enormous too

Twenty-eight hands

Every sinew of its body flowed with a matching perfect mound of muscle

He turned his beautiful muzzle around toward us and hurried his load onto his back

He had a purpose for us

My sister and daughter, I want to believe, mounted themselves,
nestling perfectly in his saddle

I pleaded to join them, but there was no space left for me

The stallion beckoned me on and I found my place behind the saddle within the comforting crook between his back and rear

In a flash we had gone and returned and he turned back and the saddled passengers knew to disembark, leaving me on

I quickly removed the saddle and was afraid I would fall off, but the stallion turned his head back toward me as though to steady me

As he began to move, I noticed my grasp tighten and his muscles flexed
so as to hold me

His whinnied laugh assured me I would not fall

The stallion was strong, safe, and confident

He turned his head and nodded and as my sister and daughter looked on

He took me away

The Trigger

I have many blessings: good family, friends, times, and a measure of intelligence, which has allowed me to rationalize about my sewers of despair. These internal and external struggles and good people have brought me to this moment in my life.

Even with the best of everything, one can land in these sewers. How can this be? In many cases it just happens. I took my failures and measured myself against others' successes. This is what drove me amok. Recently, as a Parent Teacher Organization (PTO) representative, I participated in volunteer work running a publishing center for elementary school students. I kept trying to make it better and better for the kids, but didn't realize that it was making it harder for me to live up to the expectations I was creating for myself and any future chairpersons. The purpose of volunteering got lost in a myriad of responsibilities that eventually sapped my energy levels and my aspirations. One of the main challenges with running the committee effectively was communications, particularly managing them given the district's new directive to "go green." This meant that reminders or other communications would be handled only online.

As a PTO committee, we should have been included in all PTO communications, but the new submission requirements would only allow brief, concise articles. Since our main communication encompassed an instructional overview of the publishing program, brief wasn't realistic. If the PTO board disagreed with the need for the communication, the board rejected it. The board didn't reject my articles often, but I could garner from the new tone of their guidelines that longer articles would not be feasible. We turned to the principal for assistance with our committee's needs.

Long story short, I took PTO's treatment as intentional and bottled up my frustration somewhere inside. The communication process in and of itself was exhausting, but I decided that the PTO officers were struggling with the new communications format themselves, and I shouldn't take their exclusivity-style attitude personally.

The intense workload took its toll on me and by the end of my second year running the committee, I managed to cut myself off from my co-chairs by not heeding their advice and charging ahead with my plan to change how we were going to operate the following year so as to exclude myself from the committee. I believed I had done everything possible to help the students, teachers, and PTO. In addition, my daughter would be leaving elementary school, and I would no longer be eligible to assist the committee. It was time to pass the reins to my co-chairs. They were ready.

Part of what factored into my decision was the reality that I wasn't respected by the PTO president and one of the other officers. On the contrary these women seemed to thrive on what they viewed was important PTO business such as fundraising; and, well, frankly, anything they thought was important was important and anything anyone else thought, wasn't. I concluded that they cared more about recognition than truly helping in the education of the kids.

Over the two years I chaired the publishing committee, I learned to run it without their input and became primarily concerned with what the principal wanted us to do. I finally broke down when the principal seemed to be sending signals that he wasn't going to support a year-end communications wrap-up message and a recognition assembly for the kids. Instead of taking my concerns to him directly, I e-mailed him and the PTO president. She inappropriately circulated my e-mail to other PTO members and I ended up looking like an ogre. My co-chairs became disenchanted with me and deservedly so. I didn't know how upset I had made them until the start of the following school year. We were in the cafeteria to man our booth for "Meet the Teacher" day. This day was used by PTO to educate parents about PTO committees and garner support for volunteers throughout the school year. Same day, two years earlier, I was the maverick publishing committee chair who first insisted that our committee needed its own sign-up table. I approached the principal for a table and he made sure PTO was looped into our request. The PTO president thwarted my efforts by conveniently forgetting the table. It was resolved when a former publishing committee chair offered me space at her table. Our committee needed about twenty volunteers to run the publishing program for the entire school year. If we couldn't explain the importance of literacy to parents and how our committee helped with it, we did not get the volunteer support we needed to operate effectively. Because PTO representatives seemed closed minded, I did not follow normal channels to get my table. My approach was abrasive to PTO egos so they naturally took the offensive. I really got carried away with maintaining and developing the publishing program beyond the norm.

Let's fast forward to this year. We were at a table the present chair arranged with no problem. The second chairperson was being quite snippy with me, and the reigning chair didn't seem happy to see me or appreciate my assistance even though we had previously discussed via telephone which items each planned on bringing in for the day. When the last person left the cafeteria, I forced them to come out with what was going on and why their tone of conversation was off-color. One chair quickly charged at me and spoke within inches of my face saying, "Amzy, you are sick in the mind and nasty to people." Then she told me two more times I was sick in the mind. After all the hard work we had done together two years running, I was deeply shocked. Anger rose in my cheeks. I knew this person was angry at me because I listened to her complaints but often disagreed with them because they arose from her ignorance about how to run the center. I knew she was really angry at her own ignorance. But I also knew that if I stayed to try and counter her angry accusations, I would explode and say things I would regret. So I picked up my things and left without saying a word. My body was vibrating with emotion and I was so upset that my legs shook as I walked out alone to my car. Once I got home, I was emotionally spent and as soon as I laid my head on my pillow I began to cry uncontrollably.

I was deeply saddened that my former co-chairs got so mad at me. I never wanted to offend or upset the people that had supported and helped me most. In fact, I thought I had made a lasting friend of the present chairperson. I had gone to the cafeteria that day to help and offer any future assistance I could reasonably fit into my schedule. I wanted to support her the same way she had me. I wasn't going to get the chance. I was devastated. In the end they thought I was sick in the head when in truth I had simply lost sight of what the publishing center was all about: the kids. But this was always the thought in the back of my head: if one parent was involved in the writing and language development of his/her child, that child might end up excelling in life. I knew parental involvement was instrumental in each student's success. I knew this from my personal hardships growing up. I knew this, but how could I ever get those around me to understand how vital this was? At that exact moment nobody could understand me unless someone would stand up, cut open my heart, and show the broken pieces of life left untended. I never wanted any child to go through what I did growing up. My childhood hardships got confused with just making writing fun. I had no idea making writing fun would be so politically challenging. My heartfelt desire to make something better for the kids was lost in a political battle that should never have been. Shakespearean tragedies flooded my memory, but one quote from King Lear rang clear:

...*the worst is not,*

So long as we can say, 'This is the worst.' (4.1.27)

After this event I needed to make sense of why, even when I was using my God given talents, I failed. I decided to write about my childhood in the hopes I would discover myself. I was gifted with so much more. As I remembered my father, I realized that he had it worse than I ever had and I didn't deserve to place myself in his tragic realm. My father had suffered more than I because he had nobody to reach out to and tell him they felt or understood his pain. In his world divorce was society's answer to a spouse that couldn't financially or emotionally care for himself or his family. He not only lost his livelihood, he lost his wife's love and respect, and he almost lost the love of his children. I am on the other end of this spectrum because my marital relationship is intact and stronger today than it was the day Charles and I married; and even though the kids occasionally get mad at me or at both Charles and me because of perceived unfairness, they love and respect both of us. It took me many years of soul-searching, and perhaps even writing this story, to look for and find answers to why Dad did what he did and to be able to give him back his rightful fatherly standing in my heart.

Realizing where I had gone wrong and that my errors in judgment could be rectified, I decided I had to forgive myself and ask for forgiveness from others. My father would have wanted it this way. Recognizing my own humanity allowed me to start having positive thoughts about life and face the reality of my situation. I could never make my co-chairs forgive me, and I could never make people like or be friends with me, but I could start trying to do the right things more consistently one person at a time. I also learned that even if you have a passion for something, you must never impose it on others. All or at least the majority must support the endeavor for it to truly thrive and take hold.

This is my success: learning some valuable lessons. Just like my father whose bout with alcoholism made him unapproachable, I created a wall around myself and didn't know I should get over my fear of being told "no" and just ask and see what would happen. I avoided this approach because I knew if I were unable to articulate my platform to garner support, the opportunity to help the kids would be lost. I chose to sacrifice my unstable reputation with those people that consistently had misjudged my character and motives. I chose to sacrifice my reputation with the principal because I knew he was leaving the school the following year. I chose to do all of this because I knew I was relinquishing lead chair of the committee the following year. I lost sight of who I was and how to professionally handle my responsibilities.

As I write this story, I am finding parallels between me and my father, brother, mother, friends, and acquaintances. I commune with my father's artistic abilities and the fact that he continued to persevere in terms of his relationships with his children after our parents' divorce and until his death. Like it or not, I am predominately a right-brained thinker like my mother; I think with my emotions first, and therefore the decision-making process is more challenging for me than it is for others. Like my brother I am a victim of a timeframe in my life that I cannot change and back then had no control over. I have come to accept that friends are a metaphor for acquaintances; I cannot trust them in the same way I can a member of my family. Ironically each individual poses a challenge to me to identify where the delicate balance is in terms of how each exhibits the qualities of either friend or acquaintance relative to my relationship with them. I cannot take for granted that one or two good deeds or indeed years of a seeming friendship make it so in perpetuity. Family has supplanted my friends where I find the security of both relationships almost perfectly embodied together.

I have discovered something about myself from writing this story: My character is strong because I can accommodate others' faults and let them have their moment without overreacting to them. I've learned to walk away and talk later. Even though this is extremely difficult at times, it is a vital component of salvaging relationships. Also I am equipped with the ability to reflect, examine, forgive, and persevere regardless of how badly I think I have been treated or have strayed through my conversations and interactions. I have come to realize that each time I fell short of my own expectations, I needed to forgive myself for not measuring up to my own idea of my own standards, and I absolutely need to stop comparing my failures to the successes of others. Additionally I need to strive to more objectively examine what others' say about my shortcomings or ideas.

I've discovered that writing is therapeutic, as is reading. I recently read somewhere about the six pillars of character: trustworthiness, respect, responsibility, fairness, caring, and citizenship. Using these ideals along with all the valuable lessons I have learned from personal hardships, I can try and hope to discover ways to avoid future missteps. Since my brain communicates better through my pen than through my tongue, writing may save me, especially when I need it to most. Unlike a life out of control where rats once tried to overtake me, my black stallion awaits to take me away. The best part is that unless God wills it, my writing cannot be taken away.

Life continues even when trials become so overwhelming, and you do not know how to get yourself out from under them, but somehow you do. Since I didn't know that I needed to cope with my problems as they occurred, I innocently buried my pain and fear. A single failure, after so many others, forced me to try and figure out what I was doing to repeatedly cause them. I am lucky I chose to reveal a shameful part of my life. In so doing, I was able to forgive my past, forgive myself and forgive my father. I somehow knew our lives would improve the day we moved away from the Denison house. But, I didn't know that the hardships we endured had taken an unknown toll on me. Indeed, the fears I began burying so early in life caused me to lose sight of who I was and what I wanted most from life—to be valued for who I am and for the small, positive contributions I successfully make for people that seemingly gravitate into my life and around it.

Now I know that by sharing fear, just as with grief, true healing can endure. That day has come and I now race into my future—or perhaps it is more precise to say my future is catching up to me, a stronger and, hopefully, better person.

∞ The End ∞

Epilogue

So what happened to Mom and my siblings after I left for college? Genevieve went on to a college too. She didn't finish; but she tried, and to this day I wouldn't be surprised if she ends up getting a degree after all. She is my most determined sister. Her three kids are as smart as whips. Her oldest graduated from Harvard, her second from the University of Rochester, and her youngest will do very well too, I am quite confident.

Isabelle attended two or three years of school at Penn State University, an accomplishment she should be proud of. Today she has a wonderful husband and two great kids, one in college and one not far behind.

The youngest, Tristen, moved to Texas with Mom. They spent ten years living there before Tristen married and Mom returned home. Mom ended up marrying the man who bought our Denison home. Let's call him Stan. The Denison house was sold only a few years ago. Technically, even though Stan owned it, his ex-wife lived in it through some arrangement I never asked about. Hmm, maybe I will. When Mom returned from Texas, my sister Faith mentioned Stan was in the hospital for back surgery and Mom went to visit him. Mom and Stan had hit it off to begin with, so sparks were reignited and the next thing we knew, they decided to marry. I'm happy for Mom. She and Stan have a great relationship and are happy together.

Tristen married her own guy, who since passed away from a heart attack. She has three wonderful boys, but raising her sons alone is tough on her. She seems to be managing. We all keep tabs on her and she keeps in touch when time permits.

My older siblings are doing well. They each married and had children. Sammy has four wonderful kids and I love him dearly. His experience in the juvenile facility positively impacted the rest of his life. He became a born-again and was trying to convert everyone he met to do the same. Over the years, though, he changed and converted back to Catholicism. I enjoy talking with him about faith and how God is interjecting Himself in the world we live in today. My brother is a humble truck driver and he will be with God in heaven someday. I obviously have great faith.

Speaking of faith, Faith married and followed in Mom's footsteps with the number of kids—seven—and she is already a grandmother. She converted and lives her faith as a born-again Christian. I relate to her only because she quotes scriptures that I grew up with, but applies them a little more readily and much more frequently to life than I do. I don't see her often, but when I do, we always leave each other hugging.

My oldest sister, Bonniemarie, has one boy, and her first marriage failed. That would be a whole separate story so I won't go into it here. She remarried and to the right guy the second time. She is the most successful of all of us. She started out nursing and went up the ladder as far as she could. She eventually finished her bachelor's degree and went on for her master's. She works with a company that monitors health care operations throughout the United States.

Like Amzy, I have happy memories of living with my grandma after college, and marrying the wonderful man she helped me fall in love with. I want my readers to know that many of Amzy's character traits resemble mine. Even though I lived the majority of the events in Amzy's story, many of them have been modified to suit Amzy's character. As a result, Amzy is separate and distinct. My life then is somewhat of a mystery. However, like Amzy, I tried and failed so many times, and it was always the realization of my own failures and my determination never to quit (just like pushing my tricycle up the hill at the age of three until I succeeded) that has guided me to subsequent successes. Success is not always what you thought it would be or think it is. Through every failure I learned I needed to be a better person to succeed. It never came down to doing something better or knowing better friends; it always came down to figuring out how to be a better person.

EPILOGUE

Dad did pass away at the age of fifty-three from a stroke and suffered several earlier heart attacks. His heart condition forced him to lose weight and quit drinking. He was a good man at his core, and the sewer of despair I shared with him motivated me to evaluate my life because I hoped it would help me find out who I was and what I was about. I unwittingly discovered that many of my life's experiences paralleled his. My memories of past painful events, paradoxically, helped me not only overcome some of my own pain in the here and now; but discover that what I thought was bad parenting was in reality a father who was dealing with his own failures and didn't understand that they were overtaking him. He in fact was a parent without support who as a result became depressed and unable to cope normally. I wish he were alive today to see how well his kids turned out. He would be proud of each one of us.

Made in the USA
Charleston, SC
02 July 2011